THE LOST CITY

(Joe Hawke #8)

Rob Jones

THE LOST CITY is a work of fiction. All names, characters, places and occurrences are entirely fictional products of the author's imagination or are used fictitiously. Any resemblance to current events or locales, or to persons living or dead, is entirely coincidental.

ISBN-13:978-1541124592
ISBN-10:1541124596

Other Books by Rob Jones

The Joe Hawke Series

The Vault of Poseidon (Joe Hawke #1)
Thunder God (Joe Hawke #2)
The Tomb of Eternity (Joe Hawke #3)
The Curse of Medusa (Joe Hawke #4)
Valhalla Gold (Joe Hawke #5)
The Aztec Prophecy (Joe Hawke #6)
The Secret of Atlantis (Joe Hawke #7)
The Lost City (Joe Hawke #8)

This novel is an action-adventure thriller and includes
archaeological, military and mystery themes. I welcome
constructive comments and I'm always happy to get your
feedback.

Website: www.robjonesnovels.com

Facebook: https://www.facebook.com/RobJonesNovels/

Email: robjonesnovels@gmail.com

Twitter: @AuthorRobJones

DEDICATION

For R

THE LOST CITY

PROLOGUE

The Caribbean Sea, Colombia, June 1708

With the blazing tropical sun moving rapidly toward the west, Capitan José Fernández de Santillán of the Spanish galleon San José raised a telescope to his eye and watched the horizon with a growing sense of dread. He knew the British were in the area off the coast of Cartagena, sailing in a squadron under the command of the daring Englishman Charles Wager, but where exactly was still a mystery.

But what they wanted was no mystery.

The gold.

But the British had no right to the gold because the Spanish had found it first. They had fought the Incans for it, and won. The hoard he was transporting across the oceans back to Spain was not intended for British coffers. King Philip V had been very clear in his proclamation. Santillán had heard rumors about the depressed king, and his penchant for being sung to sleep every night by the Italian castrato Farinelli, but while that was hearsay confined to the royal court, the orders about the treasure couldn't be any clearer. He was to return to Spain with the Lost Treasure of the Incas in his hold as fast as the prevailing westerlies could carry the San José, and no mistake.

And then he saw them, sailing directly toward his flotilla. He removed the scope to rub his eye and then levelled it once again at the foreign ships on the muggy horizon. For a moment he wondered if Wager had changed his strategy and was preparing to turn his ships, but then it became clear they were simply moving into battle formation and approaching his flotilla as fast as the wind would take them.

Lieutenant Commander Martinez de Medina walked up beside him and hoped his face was not conveying the fear he felt rising in his stomach. "How long, sir?"

"We should have put to sea earlier," Santillán said calmly, aware the eyes and ears of his men would be keener than ever today.

He pocketed the brass telescope and walked up the steps to the ship's forecastle. He was trying to show his men how a calm, measured commander dealt with an enemy action at sea, but inwardly he was less certain. The British enjoyed a fierce reputation at sea, inherited from centuries of dominance by the English Royal Navy. Now they were rounding on him en masse and it was time to act or he would lose everything from the gold to his reputation, and maybe even his life.

"Divide the fleet!" Santillán ordered. The swell was growing as fast as the gap between him and the British was narrowing.

The lieutenant commander looked at him nervously. "Is that wise, sir?"

"Follow my orders, commander!" the captain snapped. Moments later the order was obeyed and carried out by the helmsman. He watched with a stony, impassive glare as his small flotilla of galleons broke apart in the sultry ocean and fanned out in a defensive position.

Dividing the fleet was a questionable tactic, but Santillán knew that many of his ships were laden to the brim with the Incan treasure hoard and the British were much more powerful. Even if they suffered a defeat, at least this way some of the Treasure Fleet would get away and perhaps some small part of the lost Incan gold would stand a better chance of getting back to Madrid.

Friar Lorenzo rushed to the captain, his face a mess of tortured uncertainty. "You cannot let them get the hoard, Captain!"

"I do not intend to, Friar. Now get below decks before you get your head shot off with a cannonball." He turned away from the religious man and yelled another order as the British ships came within range. "Bring her about, Helmsman! We'll fire at her stern and rip through her that way. The planks are thinnest on her arse."

Before he could give the command to fire, the British beat him to it, and they fired with all their might and fury. Their cannonballs flew through the air and struck the San Joaquín, one of the Spanish ships to their starboard, smashing the top of her foremast clean off and tearing the rigging to shreds. Men scrambled on the deck as they struggled to contain the fire and control their vessel but Capitan Villaneuva managed to turn his ship and flee into the gathering dusk.

Santillán was pleased, but now it was their turn. "Fire!" Santillán yelled, and held on tight as the mighty cannons below fired their vengeance across the tropical waves. A second later they smashed into the starboard bow of one of the British ships.

Santillán held his telescope calmly at his eye and scanned the chaos on the British deck with amusement, but his mirth was quickly taken away when he saw them fire a renewed volley. The flash of the cannons and the rise of the smoke came first, and then a second later the thunder-deep roar as the sound raced across the ocean and struck his ears.

And then the cannonballs struck another ship in the Spanish flotilla, smashing into the stern and blasting the officers' quarters into matchwood. The destruction rained down over the water in a cloud of sea spray and smoke and men scrambled wildly on the deck to put out the fires. A second later the British fired another volley, this time punching a hole through the fore just under the portside hawsehole. It was followed a second later by an enormous explosion that blew the foredeck into the air and ripped off the bow of the ship.

"They hit the ammunition store!" Santillán said, his mouth turning downwards in a hurry. He carelessly wiped the sweat from his forehead with the silken sleeve of his shirt and took a step back toward the helm. "We need to go to their assistance at once!"

All around them now the cannonballs were smashing into their ships and exploding into enormous fireballs. A look of uncertainty flashed across the face of Lieutenant Commander Martinez de Medina. "The British outnumber us massively, sir – and it looks like they want to board us!"

Santillán turned to face him, and raised his voice. "We have men in the water so hold your tongue, man! If you think for one moment that I would abandon..."

Before he could complete his sentence, a deep, terrifying explosion roared from below their own decks and seemed to shake even the sea around them. "Oh my *God!*" Santillán said. "They've hit the powder magazines!" A second later the front of the galleon was consumed in a gigantic fireball. Smoke billowed everywhere and now the flames of the explosion were

4

licking up the mainmast and had caught on the studding sail. It was true carnage and Santillán gasped as he beheld the nightmare unfolding before him, and all under his command.

A young officer ran to him, breathless, and the panic clear on his tar-streaked face. "Sir, we're taking on water!"

Santillán stared at him for a moment and then the San José began to list badly to port. He turned to Medina. "Give the order to abandon ship!"

"Yes, sir!"

As the commander ordered sailors to prepare the skiffs and the pinnace and have the men quit the ship, Friar Lorenzo waddled up to him, his hands in a knot and his round, sweaty face a study of confused panic.

"What is it, Friar?"

"You have ordered the men off the ship!"

"Indeed, I have."

"But what about the treasure, sir?"

"The treasure shall go to the bottom of the ocean and enrich only the sharks, Friar. You will be joining it if you do not get to one of the skiffs."

"But, sir! The King has promised the church much of the treasure!"

"Then the King may swim down to the seabed and fetch it for himself!"

With the British sailing fast toward them, and the San José slowly sinking beneath the warm waves of the Caribbean Sea, Santillán's eyes crawled over the smoking, burning carnage as the ship went down, Inca gold and all. For a moment he wondered if these treasures would ever be recovered, and then he raised his eyes to the sky and offered the heavens a silent prayer.

CHAPTER ONE

Cartagena, Present Day

The Colombian sun burned over the old Colonial city without mercy. The city was established in 1533 by the Spanish who named it after Carthage, and the small bay had been a safe haven for people for five thousand years. Today, the port city was a bustling place kept alive mainly by tourism.

The Naval Del Caribe, or the Naval Museum of the Caribbean, was tucked away in the Old Town of Cartagena, deep inside the city's Sixteenth Century walls. This was one of the finest Colonial cities in all of Latin America, but none of that mattered to the man in the skull mask as he rattled through the stifling humidity of the old town's back streets in the front of an ancient Hyundai pick-up truck.

"We're almost there," he said, and clicked a fresh magazine into his Heckler & Koch MP5. "Pull your bloody masks down."

The other two men obeyed, and moments later they all had eerie Halloween masks covering their faces as they turned the final corner and pulled up across the street from the museum.

"No security on the door," said the man in a Frankenstein mask.

A third man who was wearing a Scream ghost mask turned to face the Skull. "Just as you thought, boss."

In the front seat, Skull was scanning the street ahead of him and then used the mirror to check behind. "Remember, it's in and out," he said, leaving no room for excuses later. "Then we take the object to the Syrian and go from there, right?"

"And you think you can trust the Syrian?" Frankenstein asked.

Skull didn't respond at once. The truth was he had no idea. The Syrian had come to him, not the other way around. He had spoken eloquently about his life's dream, and he reassured him that he could deliver the sort of manpower needed to achieve such a demanding mission.

The Syrian had heard about the Skull from his involvement in previous museum raids and other lootings. He now knew, the Syrian had patiently explained, where there was more gold and treasure than anywhere else on earth. More precious stones than any man could dream of in his wildest imagination.

Skull had listened and nodded in all the right places. He'd heard all the right buzzwords – Incas, lost treasure, gold, emeralds, and then even a few words that concerned him – Hezbollah, freedom-fighters, revenge… but the Syrian had made a compelling argument that only together did they have the skills to find the treasure, and he'd even spoken in hushed tones of something much more awesome lurking amongst the lost gold. Skull had reluctantly agreed to the partnership. If there was one thing he was short of it was manpower.

And as for trust… he was with Aesop, and never trusted the advice of a man in difficulties. The Syrian looked like he had more difficulties than most, but Skull had left the matter untouched. He didn't want to scare the man away with too many impertinent questions.

He turned to face Frankenstein. "Don't even trust your own reflection," he said sourly. Then he turned to the bound and gagged man on the back seat. "Wouldn't you agree with that?"

The man looked back at Skull with fear in his eyes but made no reply due to the gag tied around his mouth. The many beatings the young man had received at the hands of Skull and his friends had taught him not to aggravate these men, and now he sat in passive silence. He dreamed of escaping from their grip, but his value to them was too great, and they never let him out of their sight.

A hard jab in his ribs knocked him from his daydream and he was suddenly aware the other men were all now laughing at his inability to reply on account of the gag.

"I thought you'd agree," Skull said, turning in his seat and knocking him out with the butt of his weapon. He twisted back around and turned to the masked men. "Let's go."

Skull checked the mask was secure and they jumped out of the van. Their rehearsal paid off when they were through the lobby and up the stairs in less than thirty seconds leaving only two dead security guards behind them.

They scanned the museum's upper level for any sign of the target and their hunt was cut short when their prey saw them and tried to get away.

"There he is!" Frankenstein said, pointing at the door at the end of the corridor. A man in a linen jacket had already seen them and was moving toward the door with speed. "We need him alive!"

Skull directed his men forward and they thundered down the short museum corridor with their submachine guns. A woman with a pair of glasses balanced on her nose opened her door to see what all the fuss was about but after seeing the guns she thought better of it and disappeared back inside her office.

*

Héctor Barrera slammed the door, turned the key in the lock and stood up against the wall as he strained for breath. His asthma was exacerbated by stress and now his heart was beating nineteen to the dozen as his panicked mind raced in a bid to evade his pursuers.

He knew who they were, and he had been expecting them – but not like this. He had visualized a business meeting. A cosy chat and a simple transaction. You get the mask, and I get the brown envelope stuffed with hundred dollar bills. After a few short breaths he could feel his chest tighten and the sound of his high-pitched wheezing now filled the silent room.

"Give us the mask," the voice said in Spanish. Barrera thought the accent sounded Mexicano but with a tinge of Guatemalan around the edges. He couldn't be sure but the man was certainly not a local. Then another man's voice – this time speaking in English.

"We know you have it, old man. Hand it over and we will let you live."

The second voice was gravelly but clearer – Dutch, or New Zealand, maybe – but before his mind could think about it any further there was a crash at the door and he felt it judder in the frame. He heard some swearing and then he felt someone kick the lower panel of the door but it held in place.

"Last chance and we do it the hard way," the gravelly voice said.

Barrera's mind raced again as he strained to think of a way out. Opposite him on the far wall of the office was the window, but he was on the third floor and there was no fire escape. Nothing beyond that glass except a long drop to the asphalt and a very hard landing.

"Who are you?" he said, stalling for time. "What do you want with me?"

"You know who we are, Barrera – don't play us for fools. We want the mask from the galleon and we know you have it."

Before he could reply there was more swearing and then a gunshot. He nearly jumped out of his skin as the bullet tore through the upper panel a few inches from his head and buried itself in his map of Colombia on the wall beside the window.

"Okay... okay – it's here! Please don't kill me."

"Waste a bullet on you?" Skull said.

The door began to open and Skull helped it on its way with a violent kick of his boot. It smacked open so hard it began to wobble shut again requiring a second kick. Barrera walked backwards in fear, clutching a golden mask to his chest as if it would make him bullet proof. He was horrified to see they were wearing masks – a skull, a Frankenstein monster and a ghost, and all carrying guns.

The man in the front took off his skull mask and stared at the ancient artefact, his dark eyes settling on the glittering golden mask in the academic's shaking hands.

"You!" Barrera said.

"I see you have it," Skull said.

"It wasn't easy getting it out of the vaults – please... I've done everything you asked of me."

"This is true," Skull said snatching the mask from him. "You have done everything I need you to do for me."

A nervous smile played on Barrera's trembling lips. "And the settlement?"

"I need you to do one more thing for me, Héctor."

"Anything!"

10

Skull gave a grim smile and raised his pistol. "Die."

"No!"

The shot rang out in the tiny office, and Héctor Barrera staggered backwards into his desk. He turned and tried to hang on to the desk in a bid to stop himself going over, but it was in vain. The searing pain in his chest and the loss of blood pressure forced him down to the cheap vinyl tiles of his office, and then he was on his side, staring up at the world in agony.

He watched the man with the Skull mask step over to him with the gun from his new sideways angle, reaching out with a shaking hand in a desperate last-minute plea for his life, but he received no mercy – only a second bullet.

"There's your bastard settlement," the man said, pulling the Skull mask back on, and slammed the door behind him as his life slipped away into darkness.

CHAPTER TWO

Elysium

Joe Hawke turned around to take one last look at the gravestone and shook his head in disbelief. Maria Kurikova was dead, and Ryan Bale was missing presumed dead. Hawke preferred Missing in Action because at least that way it left some hope for his survival, however slim. Far away across the Atlantic Ocean, their leader Sir Richard Eden was lying in a London hospital deep in a coma. His condition had deteriorated badly on board the USS Harry S. Truman and he'd been flown straight to London.

To complete the shattering of their team, Alex Reeve was in Washington DC in a military hospital due to a bullet wound in her shoulder. One of them men from the Black Hawk had not got back to the chopper and survived the F18 missile strike. He'd tried to take out Alex with his assault rifle and wounded her, but Kim Taylor had taken him down with a double tap from behind the cover of the black smoke pouring from the chopper's wreckage.

She'd told him that she was going to have to go back anyway. While she was on the aircraft carrier she had been recalled by her father due to his new position as President-elect of the United States. Having won the election in early November, it was no longer considered safe to have his family drifting around the world due to fears of kidnapping and blackmail.

Alex would recover and get stronger, and he had hopes Richard Eden would do the same, but what was crushing Hawke was Ryan and Maria. He was struggling with the sense of injustice and rage more than he thought was possible for someone with a past as rocky and violent as his. He had watched many good friends die in battle, and even more fall to PTSD or the bottle, but watching a young couple taken away like this had really got to him.

He sighed and stared up at the complex that used to be Elysium Headquarters, but was now no more than a burned-out husk. He could still hardly bring himself to believe what Alex had told them about the Apache attack and the squad of Special Forces men who landed in the Black Hawk on north beach. It all seemed like something from a nightmare. He had no idea how long it would take them to pull the place together, but he knew they had to try. It was their home, and at least some of the lower floors were still intact.

He wandered away from the grave, picked up his kukri knife and resumed sharpening the Nepalese Army weapon, filing the edge of the blade with a butcher's steel.

Lea walked over and sat down beside him on the small bench a few yards from the freshly dug earth. The Irishwoman kept her eyes closed as the swaying palms above her head broke the sunlight up and cast mottled shadows on her smooth face. "So what now?"

"I'm not giving up on him," Hawke said. "Not until I know for sure."

"Joe…"

He looked at the graves again: Olivia Hart, Sophie Durand, Bradley Karlsson, Ben, Alfie, Sasha and now Maria. The list grew longer. Their sacrifices were all marked here in the center of Elysium, their secret base, shaded by the palms. It was the one area that got away totally unscathed from the vicious assault on the island.

He tried to fight it, but the thought of Ryan's grave now manifested in his mind, right there beside the others. No... not until I know for sure," he whispered.

He looked out to sea and saw Cairo Sloane speeding across the waves on her windsurfing board. A bright flash of scarlet against the dazzling turquoise ocean. This place didn't feel like paradise anymore.

Lea saw his eyes as they tracked Scarlet across the water. "Nothing seems to affect her, not in the way it does the rest of us."

"Cairo Sloane is in a different category," he said almost automatically, and then with more feeling: "I wouldn't have been able to get to that bastard Matheson without Maria. She was the one who shone the light on all that for me. I owe her so much, and now she's gone."

Lea raised a hand and laid it gently on his arm. "It's not your fault, Joe."

"If not mine, then whose?" he said, raising his voice more than he meant. "I was the one leading the operation. I put her in that place. She was following *my* orders when she was killed. This is just Sophie and Olivia all over again."

"We're not kids, Joe. We all know the risks. Maria was a very experienced FSB agent. You can't take that away from her. When you say it's all your fault you're just saying she wasn't capable of making her own decisions."

Hawke said nothing, but moved her arm away and rose to his feet. She was right, of course. Maria Kurikova wasn't a child. She was a highly competent agent for the Russian security services and a respected member of the ECHO team. She lived the way she wanted, and she died doing something she loved, but none of that made it any easier on Hawke and his tortured mind.

The mind that was now racing with the terrible events of the Seastead and his failure to kill the mysterious Oracle. Knowing Dirk Kruger and Dragan Korać were both dead brought almost no comfort at all considering the price their deaths had cost the team. Not even Reaper taking Kamchatka out or Maria sending Luk to such a miserable and violent death could bring any sense of fairness or balance to the world given the terrible loss they had suffered with the deaths of Ryan and Maria.

Maria. Since the now-notorious Seastead battle he had felt hollowed out, struck by her death like never before. He didn't want to ask himself why he'd reacted in this way, that maybe he'd felt something more for her than mere friendship. He knew he loved Lea, so maybe it was just that he was drifting too far from his Special Forces days and could no longer deal with death in the way they'd trained him to all those years ago. But on top of Liz, it just felt like someone was twisting the knife. He couldn't bring himself to think about what might happen if Lea ever got hurt.

Hawke loved Lea. At least he thought he did. It was a complicated business. At least it had become a complicate business since the death of Maria Kurikova. And then there was Alex Reeve. He was no fool. He knew the way the American felt about him, or at least he thought he did. When it came to successfully receiving signals from women, he liked to think he was the best among men, but the truth was he had no more idea than any other man and he knew it. Still, when they had been together in Idaho in her father's mountain cabin he had been certain she was trying to be more than friends.

He was silent for a long time. When he spoke, it was through gritted teeth. "Otmar Wolff is a dead man walking."

"If we ever see him again," Lea said with a sigh.

"You can count on that," he said. "I don't care how long it takes. Wolff will pay for all of this."

Lexi Zhang emerged from the headquarters building and called Lea over. Someone wanted to speak with her on the phone. As she got up to leave she kissed Hawke on the cheek before walking away.

He watched her step inside the shade of the wrecked building and tried to use the silence to get some perspective but then Scarlet walked up the beach toward him. Her hair was slicked back with the ocean and the saltwater was running off her wetsuit. She stepped across the hot sand and smiled at him.

"Are you sure you're not putting on weight?" she asked, but he could tell from the tone it was a half-hearted attempt to lighten the mood. "Just looks a little *doughy* down there."

"I just keep thinking about all the ways I could have done things differently and then they would still be alive and maybe even Rich would be okay."

"Blaming yourself for Ryan and Maria is stupid," she said quietly. "But blaming yourself for the attack on this island is downright idiotic. What the hell could you have done differently to stop it? We don't even know who did it."

"We know they were Americans."

"Alex *thinks* they might have been American, Joe. A big difference."

"It's something to go on."

"If you say so."

He paused a moment, watching the surf crash on the beach. "How's Camacho these days?"

"If you must know we're getting along."

"Is the great Cairo Sloane finally settling down?"

"I wouldn't go that far, darling. Let's just say I can see a future for myself that doesn't involve…"

"Boozing, smoking and fighting?"

"I was going to say a future that doesn't involve being lonely, if you must know."

"I'm pleased for you, Cairo. You know I am."

"And what about the great Josiah Hawke?" she asked mischievously.

"What do you mean?"

"Are we looking at a Mrs Lea Hawke one day?"

Her words made him pause for a moment. He had never heard Lea described like that before – with his own name. He had never put the names together in his own mind before and it sounded strange. It brought back memories of his first wife and their wedding day.

"Well, if you must know, I was…"

He stopped talking when the sun flashed on the door to reveal Lea and Lexi as they emerged from the ruined compound. Reaper was a step behind. They both watched them step outside and walk over to the garden.

Scarlet lit a cigarette. "You can tell me later darling."

"That was weird," said Lea, sitting back down beside Hawke.

"What was weird?" Scarlet said, blowing a cloud of smoke into a mosquito and sending it into a rapid u-turn.

"The phone call I just had. It was someone named Magnus Lund."

"Shit," Scarlet said. "That *is* weird."

Lea rolled her eyes and sighed. "If you'll let me *finish*, then I can properly explain the weirdness. Mr Lund was calling me from on board a jet over the Atlantic."

"Not even vaguely weird yet," Scarlet said, dragging on her cigarette and pulling her hat down over her face to block the sun.

"He's on board a flight from Copenhagen to Miami, where he wants us to meet with him about something he described as urgent."

"Do we even know who this bloke is?" Hawke said.

"We do," Lea said with a broad smile, "because he just told me. Apparently, now Rich is in hospital, Magnus Lund is the leader of the Consortium that owns this island."

CHAPTER THREE

Miami

"I thought this place was supposed to be sunny?" Hawke said as he opened up the umbrella he'd bought in the airport. People were bustling all around them as they made their way along Brickell Avenue until they reached the address Lund had given them.

They crossed the lobby and took the elevator to the top floor. When the doors slid silently open they revealed a hardwood corridor bereft of decoration. They stepped out of the elevator and walked toward the only door, and Lea tapped gently on the panelled wood.

"Enter."

They walked into a large light-filled space and took in the opulence. It was postmodern in style, and expensively decorated with abstract art and sculpture, and on the floor was an enormous ushak rug. Behind the desk, a man in a sober suit but no neck tie flipped his laptop screen down and looked up at them. His face was lean and he wore a pair of frameless glasses.

"Good day – please take a seat."

They exchanged a glance and did as he asked, each taking a comfortable leather seat opposite his big desk.

"I'm Magnus Lund. Would you like coffee?" he asked.

"Not for me," Scarlet said, peering around the room for a drinks cabinet.

"I don't mind if I do," said Hawke, trying to get the measure of the man.

19

Lea smiled at him. "I'd love one, thanks."

Lund spoke in Danish into the intercom on his desk and then returned his attention to the five ECHO members sitting opposite him.

"Out with it then," Hawke said.

Lund stared back at him, expressionless. "Out with what?"

"Who are you?" Lea said.

"I already told you, my name is Lund."

"Yeah, we got that part," Hawke said. "I meant, who are the Eden Consortium?"

"Of course you did," Lund said, smiling. "The Eden Consortium was established by Sir Richard to provide funding to run the fun and games you have down in the Caribbean."

"Fun and games?" Hawke said. "We've lost some good people."

"My apologies – a poor choice of words on my part. I mean to say only that we are a small group of international backers with a similar worldview. After the attack on the island and the hospitalization of Sir Richard we convened at once and I have asked you here to express our sympathies."

"That's very kind of you," Hawke said sarcastically. "But what's the real reason we're here?"

Lund gave Hawke a thoughtful look and leaned forward closer to the desk. He rested his elbows on the desktop and then steepled his fingers. "I see you are an astute observer of human nature so let me get right down to it. Sir Richard is in a coma, but that doesn't mean we're off the job. A few hours ago a museum in Colombia was raided by three masked men."

"Sounds like trouble," Scarlet said, lighting a cigarette before the sentence had even left her mouth.

"Yes, but what sort of trouble?" Reaper asked.

Lund leaned back into his chair, his face draining of what little color it had. "You might recall a galleon that the Colombians discovered off their coast last year?"

Hawke nodded. "The San José?"

Lund nodded.

"I remember that," Scarlet said. "They just brought a shit load of treasure up out of it and carted it off to a museum in Cartagena."

"Gripping stuff," Hawke said.

"But where's the trouble?" said Lea.

"As I said, the museum just got raided by a group of highly professional men."

Hawke sat up in his chair and looked at him sharply. "Treasure hunters?"

"They weren't looking for ice creams, Joe," Scarlet said with a sigh.

"We don't know who they were," Lund said coolly.

"You know, I'm not sure if I can bring myself to give a shit about any of this," Lea said in response. "Not any more."

Lund looked at her sharply but it was Hawke who answered. "We owe it to Maria, Ryan and Rich to give a shit," he said firmly. "And that's exactly what we're going to do. What I want to know now is – who raided that museum and why?"

Reaper shifted in his chair and gave a grunt of dissatisfaction. "And what did they take?"

"That's easy," Lund said. "It's not public knowledge but I have my contacts. They stole only one item."

This captured everyone's attention, even Scarlet's, and now they were all fixing their eyes on the sombre Dane.

"Only one item?" Hawke said.

"What was it?" asked Lexi.

"Something that was discovered in the hoard in the wreckage of the San José – a small golden mask."

"Curiouser and curiouser," Lea said.

"Exactly what I'm thinking," said Lexi.

Hawke stood up from his seat. "Any more details on this mask?"

Lund sighed. A bridge of trust had not yet formed between them but he had no choice. "The Mask of Inti is an ancient Incan facemask made of pure gold which depicts Inti, the Incan god of the sun. Believed by many archaeologists to have been merely a legend until recently discovered on the wrecked ship, the mask is supposed to hold a clue leading to the…" He stopped talking and studied their faces for a few moments. The atmosphere in the plush office was tense and awkward.

"Leading to where?" Lexi asked.

"Yes, don't keep us all in suspenders, *dahling*."

"There are few details, naturally – the Incas never left written records as far as we can tell, but my contact in Colombia, a Héctor Barrera, believed that there was some kind of legend saying that the mask would lead the bearer of it to the Lost City of the Incas."

"The Lost City of the Incas?" Lea said.

"Yes," Lund said curtly. "Paititi."

"I thought that was just a…" Hawke said.

"Just a what?" Lund said.

"I was going to say just a myth, but then I realized that being just a myth doesn't mean much anymore."

"No," the Dane replied flatly. "People have sought the Lost City for literally hundreds of years, but every expedition has ended in total failure, and very often the deaths of those taking part. The main problem was always a lack of reliable information detailing its location, but now it looks like there might be a new lead."

"The mask?" Lea asked.

"Yes. According to Professor Barrera, there were legends about the Mask of Inti pointing the way to Paititi, but the truth is until we found the San José off the coast, the mask itself was no more than a legend."

Lea sighed and fixed her eyes on Lund. "And this Barrera is certain the mask is the real deal – the genuine Mask of Inti?"

Lund nodded slowly. "Of that there is no doubt. He had a short time with the artefact before the raid, and was most certain of its authenticity. It was found with a number of other items on the San José that he was sure were once part of the famous Lost Treasure of the Incas, and he was the very best. We can be certain we're looking for the genuine article."

"He *was* the very best?" Hawke asked.

Lund's face turned into a stern frown. "I'm afraid he was shot by the looters in the raid and rushed to hospital, but he was dead on arrival."

"Do we have any leads?" Reaper asked. He knew they all felt the same thing he did – that the one person they needed more than anyone just wasn't here anymore.

"That is where you come in," Lund replied. "I have arranged for you to meet with a Professor Meier in Cartagena. He holds a senior position at the museum that was looted and has more details of the raid."

"Looks like we're off again," Scarlet said.

"And soon," Lund replied. "You're meeting Meier later this afternoon so I suggest you fly immediately."

And with that, they were on their way.

CHAPTER FOUR

Cartagena

Luis Moyano was a freshly-minted doctor of archaeology from the Universidad de los Andos in Bogotá with a PhD so fresh you could still smell the wrapping. It might be true that Luis had about as much life experience as the average boy scout, but that wasn't about to stop him taking on the world, no sir. His new job at the naval museum was just the first step in what he hoped would be a long and eminent career.

Now, he looked at the people standing outside his office door, wiped his hand on his shirt and offered it to them.

"I was expecting Professor Meier," Lea said, reluctantly taking the hand.

"And I was expecting the police," he said. "They're talking to everyone about the robbery."

Hawke stepped up. "We're investigating the same crime."

Lea showed him her ID card. "Is Professor Meier here?"

"No. Unfortunately Ricardo was taken ill a few hours ago and went home. I'm afraid he won't be able to help you, but he was my supervisor for several years and my boss here so I know him better than anyone... except Mrs Meier, of course." Without waiting for a response from the others Luis exploded into the most awkward laugh Lea had ever heard in her life.

She glanced at Hawke for a second and then back to Luis. "Can we come in?"

"Ah, yes... of course. Forgive me." Luis walked backwards a few steps into his office and tripped over his bin, knocking pieces of paper and some crumpled soda cans onto the floor. "Paila!" he said, and immediately dropped to his knees to pick it all back up again. "Please, take a seat while I sort this mess out."

Lea and Hawke exchanged a glance. "No, you're all right, mate." Hawke said, raising his eyebrow as he watched the young man scrabbling about on the floor. "I prefer to stand."

A minute later and Luis Moyano was on his feet again and moving back around to his desk. "So, I would be happy to help any friend of Ricardo's – as you can see, I have researched this field extensively." As he spoke he wafted his arms to indicate his vast collection of peer-reviewed journals and books, but along the way he knocked over his coffee cup and it slopped out all over a pile of students' papers. "Oh, damn it all!"

As Luis began to mop up the mess with his pocket handkerchief, Hawke rolled his eyes and leaned in to Lea. "Is this guy for real?" he whispered.

"Shhh," she said, and slapped him away.

"So," Luis said, smiling broadly as he stuffed the coffee-soaked cloth back into his pocket. "How can I help you?"

"We're here about the robbery at the museum," Hawke said flatly.

Luis shook his head and sighed. "We're all very angry and shaken up. I hope Héctor is all right after such a terrible ordeal."

"You mean you haven't heard?" Lea said.

"Heard what? I was in the library researching all morning with strict instructions not to be interrupted."

Hawke sighed and moved forward a step. "Héctor Barrera was murdered during the raid."

"Señor Barrera is dead?" Luis's mouth fell open in shock. "We were told he was injured and taken to hospital."

"That's true, but he died before he got there. I'm sorry," Lea said. "Did you know him well?"

"We weren't close at all, no… but I knew him a little professionally. I worked with him on several projects involving the Inca culture not to mention the discovery of the San José." Luis fell into his chair and ran a hand through his hair. "I can't believe this."

"I think the San José is why he was killed," Lea said.

Luis looked up at her. "Really? What makes you say that?"

"Tell me," Hawke said, "Do you have a manifest of the treasure items found on board the galleon?"

"Somewhere, yes. Let me look for it." Luis jumped up from his desk and turned to search the filing cabinet. He tried to open the top drawer but it was stuck, so he pulled harder, and then harder again. Turning to face Lea and Hawke with an embarrassed look on his face he grinned and made his apologies. "It's not locked – just a stuck a bit."

Hawke glanced at Lea and sighed. They were both watching the spider plant on top of the cabinet as it wobbled back and forth, and expecting the inevitable.

Luis gave it a serious yank this time and sent the plant flying through the air. Lea reached out and caught it and Hawke gave a round of applause, but the soil went everywhere.

Lea handed the plant back. "Luis?"

"Yes?"

"Is that the key right there?' She pointed to a lone key sitting on top of a little pad of Post-It notes.

"Ah – yes, perhaps. I thought it was unlocked!"

Hawke and Lea exchanged another glance. "All we want is a quick look at the manifest," Lea said, trying not to laugh behind the young man's back as Hawke re-enacted her catching the spider plant.

"Of course," Luis said. "I will get it for you now the cabinet is unlocked. I don't know what made me think it was already unlocked. Professor Gomez came in here earlier and asked for something and I was sure I had already unlocked it."

"Have you found it yet?" Hawke asked.

"Yes! Here it is. The manifest from the San José!"

He pulled out a folder from the cabinet and spun around, smashing his elbow on the top of the drawer and cursing loudly as he rubbed it with his hand.

Lea took the manifest and opened it up. She traced her finger down the long list of items on the paper as Hawke peered over her shoulder.

"Look at all this stuff," she said.

"Don't pretend you know what any of it is," Hawke said, nudging her gently in the ribs.

"Get lost, Josiah," she said with a smile. "Ah ha – I found it!"

Her finger pointed at the Mask of Inti and Hawke nodded as he looked at it. "So it's real all right. What can you tell us about this mask, Luis?"

"It's small – like a child's mask – and made of solid gold of the highest quality. It has some precious stones embedded in it but of more interest are the markings."

"Markings?"

"I can say no more because I only know what Héctor told me. I never actually saw the mask myself."

"But why do you think these markings are so important?"

He smiled at them. "I know what you're thinking. You're thinking the markings will lead you to the Lost City of the Incas. This is what those murdering thieves must be thinking. I have heard the legend too."

"You're sceptical?"

"I am not sceptical at all," he replied. "I am absolutely certain the markings will not lead to any great lost city for the simple reason I do not believe there is such a place. So no scepticism – just certainty."

"But Héctor believed in the Lost City," Lea said.

Luis nodded and frowned sadly. "Héctor lived on a cloud of farts – is that how you say it in English?"

"Not exactly ringing any bells," Hawke said.

"I mean he is – how do you say – out of touch with reality?"

Hawke smiled. "That's more like it but I preferred the first way you said it."

"It's true though – he had some insane theories about the Incas and the Nazca Lines that very nearly got him fired on more than one occasion. He certainly believed in the Lost City, but that isn't to say such a place existed. Just because he was an eminent archaeologist does not mean he was always right or all his theories are sure to be true."

"We need to find out one way or the other," Lea said.

"So how can I help?"

"First thing we need to find out is who exactly knocked this place off," Hawke said. "Do you have any idea?"

Luis shook his head. "Not at all – the police are still investigating as you must have seen when you walked to my office. They've been here all day. Perhaps we should talk with them?"

Hawke moved toward the door. "I think that sounds like a grand idea."

CHAPTER FIVE

Luis Montoya walked them along the corridor until they reached the young police officer guarding Barrera's office. A short conversation later and they were walking down the steps to the museum's security office where a large, bald man with a thick moustache introduced himself as Lieutenant Rodrigo Santos.

He checked their ID, and not content with that he made some calls. When he padded back into the small office he gave a cursory nod and told them to sit.

"The Major says you check out, so you can stay."

"That's very kind of him," Hawke said.

Santos stared at him with weary eyes and sighed. "You prefer my men to take you to jail for obstructing the investigation?"

Lea scowled at Hawke. "We're very grateful to be here, Lieutenant, and we'd like to help in any way we can."

Santos paused a few seconds before responding and then nodded his head, crumpling up his double chin. "Good," he said, and pointed at Luis. "And *he* stays outside. He's a potential suspect."

Inside the small office, Santos flicked on a monitor and sighed. "We have only this footage from the CCTV." He spun around and replayed the black and white film on the security monitor. "I've watched it fifty times. Perhaps you can be of more help."

Hawke and Lea stared at the grainy image as it flickered to life. "What do they use for a camera?" Hawke asked, squinting at the screen. "A potato?"

Santos gave him a look. "Not a potato, no. A *camera*."

"Right."

"You can see there were three of them, and they wore these stupid Halloween masks for nearly the entire raid."

Lea stepped forward, searching the fuzzy image for anything that might help her. "Nearly?"

"Yes... what our murderers didn't know was there is also a camera just across the street on a restaurant. While the museum's internal CCTV shows us nothing, when they clambered into the van one of them took his mask off just a second too early."

"Can we see it?" Lea asked.

Santos sighed and turned his round face to her. "What do you think I'm doing now?"

"Sorry."

The Lieutenant changed the discs and played the back-up CCTV footage from the restaurant. The image was black and white but of a much higher quality this time and it was easy to make out various details as they watched the footage. A handful of pedestrians were walking along the pavement and then the men burst into shot. They were all holding guns and wearing the masks Santos had described a few moments ago. They ran toward a Hyundai and Hawke noticed someone was slumped in the back seat.

They pushed the passers-by roughly out of the way and opened the doors of their van. They clambered into it and that was when one of the men ripped off his mask.

Hawke was stunned when he looked at the CCTV footage and saw the unmistakable face of Dirk Kruger appear from behind the skull mask. At first he thought he was imagining it but then Lea spoke.

"Holy Buggering Moses – is that Dirk Kruger?"

Hawke clenched his jaw and felt his blood pressure rising. "It damn well is."

His eyes burned two holes in the screen as he watched Kruger jump into the Hyundai and skid off down the street. "Rewind it."

Santos complied. "Who is this Kruger?"

"He's a professional shit," Lea said.

Hawke was speechless. He thought Kruger had died on the Oracle's Seastead in the same devastating explosion that had killed Ryan. That day had been chaos – his memory of it just a blur of sea spray, gunfire and the noxious smoke of battle as they fought to stop the Oracle fleeing, but at least he thought he had come to terms with it all. This raised it all in his heart and mind. "Tell me I'm not seeing a ghost," he mumbled.

Lea gripped his arm. "You're not seeing a ghost."

Hawke's eyes widened. "Don't you realize what this means? If Kruger is alive then maybe Ryan is too."

Lea shook her head. "That's a helluva leap, Joe. It was crazy out there that day and you heard what Reaper said about the explosion. Maybe Kruger just got lucky – besides, if Ryan had survived he would have contacted us by now to stop us worrying."

But Hawke's optimism was undeterred. "Yes – unless Kruger got to him after the explosion. Maybe he's holding him hostage with a view to using his life as leverage against us."

Lea furrowed her brow. "You really cared about him, didn't you?"

Hawke clenched his jaw and was silent for a moment. "He was under my command – a civilian that I let go into a dangerous military environment with a hostile enemy. I have a responsibility to make sure he's all right. It's every commander's duty. Now there's a chance, at least and…"

"He's *dead*, Joe. You have to accept that. Maria's gone too, and for all we know Rich isn't going to make it. Remember what you told me? We owe them and we repay that debt by not stopping, by keeping on and taking out bastards like Kruger. With Rich in a coma it's up to us to lead ECHO now – it's up to you."

"Me? You're the 2IC."

Santos stared up at them with a bemused face.

"I'm Second In Command in name only, Joe, and we both know it. Ever since you came on board it's always been you leading the team when we're in the field."

He sighed as he listened to her words. The truth was he felt used-up, especially after the loss of so many team members during the Seastead battle. Their decimated team was no longer a place of camaraderie and banter, but a hollowed-out crew of grieving friends. They had come so far together, only to lose so much at what they had thought was the final hurdle, but was in reality just the beginning of a terrible new nightmare.

Destroying the Oracle and his mad cult of immortals would have been a tall order before their team was annihilated, but now with only a handful of them left they stood no chance. They would be lucky if they could stop a madman like Kruger from pillaging the Lost Treasure of the Incas, never mind the sort of force the mysterious Oracle could muster to guard his desperate secret.

"I don't know any more…"

"What happened to never give in and never give up?" she asked, rubbing his arm.

"It gave in and gave up."

"Stop talking shite, ya skanger. What is it you always say – where's your spirit of adventure?"

"I've never said that."

She rolled her eyes. "Get out of it! It was one of the first things you ever said to me back on that night when we chasing that little toerag over the rooftops of Geneva. Remember?"

"Of course I remember, you silly goose."

"Silly *what* now?"

"I said, let's get our arses into gear and get after that bastard Kruger."

"That's more like the Josiah Hawke I know and love."

"Don't push it, Donovan."

She smiled and was pleased to see he was perking up again. "So what now?"

"Well, not only do we know what they've got, but now we also know who's behind it – Dirk Kruger. In my book that gives us plenty more to go on than we usually have, so let's get cooking."

She kissed him on the cheek. Hawke was back again.

Santos cleared his throat and gave them both the evil eye. "If it's fine with you two, I have an investigation to lead. Who did you say was wearing the skull mask?"

"His name's Dirk Kruger," Hawke said.

"And what can you tell me about him?"

"He'd rather you caught him than I did."

*

They walked away from the museum and met up with Scarlet, Lexi and Reaper who were all sitting in the terrace of a café drinking coffees. Hawke was surprised to see Luis Montoya had joined them and was laughing like a distressed donkey at something Reaper had said.

"So what did Lieutenant Columbo have to say?" Scarlet asked.

"It's not what he said," Lea said. "It's what he showed us. It shocked the shit out of both of us."

"Dirty old bastard," Scarlet said. "I'm sure there's a way to complain about that sort of thing."

Hawke stared at her. "Really?"

"Sorry. I just cannot stop myself."

"Said the vicar to the actress," Lea said.

"Not you too," Scarlet said.

"It was Kruger," Hawke said flatly.

Three shocked faces stared back at him.

"That *is* shocking," Scarlet said. "Probably even more so than if old Santos really had exposed himself and showed you his old chap."

"Does this mean Ryan is alive?" Lexi asked.

"Yes." Hawke said.

"No, not necessarily," Lea said. "Let's not get excited. There are a dozen reasons why Kruger could have survived the explosion and Ryan didn't."

"No... I know that was him in the back of the Hyundai."

"Kruger..." Reaper said through gritted teeth. "But I watched him die!"

"Obviously not, Vincent," Lexi said.

"But what the hell is the little bastard up to with that mask?" Scarlet asked.

"That's what we need to find out," Hawke said. "But whatever it is, it's not going to be good. I think we know enough about him now to know Rich wasn't kidding when he said he was the luckiest bastard he'd ever met."

"And the most unpredictable," Lexi added.

"Who the hell is Kruger?" asked Luis.

Scarlet finished her coffee, lit a cigarette and lowered her sunglasses. "Never you mind."

"He's an old enemy of ours," Hawke said, glancing at Scarlet. "And I think we might need your help in tracking him down."

"My help?" Luis said, smiling proudly.

"And the assistance of one Alex Reeve, currently resident in Washington DC."

"Alex?"

He nodded. "Now we know that sack of shit is in Colombia, we can start tracking him but we can't do that without Alex's help."

"Is she up to it?" Lexi asked.

"Of course she's up to it," Scarlet said. "She only got a nine mil in the shoulder. She must be bored off her arse."

"Yes, quite," Hawke said, looking at all of his friends and seeing the first flicker of hope since the Seastead. "Let's get Ryan back."

CHAPTER SIX

The four-hundred mile flight to Bogotá crossed almost due-south over the top half the country and Hawke peered down with a distinct lack of interest at the vast agricultural lands beneath their jet – cotton, yams, cassava. Since the Seastead battle he had found it hard to raise an interest in anything and he doubted Colombian banana plantations would bring him back to the surface, but now he had a new hope, and that drove him onwards like jet fuel.

Not only was he now certain Ryan was alive, but Alex Reeve had worked her magic and found out that Dirk Kruger had taken a flight from Cartagena to Bogotá, the country's capital city. He had flown alone. The two goons in the raid were Cartagena locals paid for the robbery and no more. When he landed he met with two other men in an obscure hotel. Alex hacked the hotel's CCTV and had images.

Now, her voice was faint and crackly, but he could hear her clear enough as he stared at the pictures of Kruger and the two men. They were sitting in the hotel bar sharing drinks in tall glasses. "So who are these toerags?" he asked.

"The guy in the black shirt you already know as Dirk Kruger, I believe."

"You can say that again... and the others?"

"The dude in the beard is Ziad Saqqal, a former military commander with the Syrian Army who defected to the rebels a few months ago."

"This is a bad start, Alex. Please make the next few words relaxing and peaceful."

"Sorry, no can do. The other guy with the glasses is Dr Bashir Jawad."

"Please tell me he's the Syrian national backgammon champion or something like that."

"More disappointment coming your way, Josiah. Jawad may or may not play backgammon, but his day job is at the Department of Bacteriology and Parasitology at the American University of Beirut in Lebanon. He's a leading bacteriologist with a lot of respect in the academic community."

"What was wrong with the backgammon thing?"

"You wanted the truth. Are you saying you can't *handle* the truth?"

Hawke smiled for a moment, pleased to see they hadn't destroyed her sense of humor, but his face quickly dropped back into a frown when he remembered what she had said about Saqqal and Jawad. "Bacteriology?"

"This has to be something to do with weaponization, Joe."

"Yeah... and here I was thinking we were busy enough trying to catch Kruger, rescue Ryan and save the Lost Treasure of the Incas. Now we have a couple of psychos with a bioweapon fixation on our hands."

"Yup."

"What else have you got on Saqqal?"

"Not a whole lot, but enough to grease the wheels. In his younger days he was in the Syrian Army where he rose through the ranks with some efficiency until becoming a highly respected general, but that's where things went wrong. No one knows why but he left the army and ended up joining Hezbollah where his talents were put to use serving as a strategist and field commander in its military arm."

"Don't stop now," he said sarcastically. "I can hardly contain myself."

"He went back into Syria a few years ago with his Hezbollah troops where he fought to defend Assad against the rebels, but then returned to Lebanon when he was wounded in the arm. It was then he hooked up with Bashir Jawad and a beautiful relationship was born."

"Certainly sounds like it. What about this Jawad toerag?"

"He's easy – he has a very public profile from his work at the university. A little older than Saqqal and zero military experience. Educated in Lebanon and France with post-doctoral work in the US, he's worked in the field of bacteriology for decades and is considered a world authority on the subject."

"And for some reason these two clowns are hanging around with Dirk Kruger and they're all searching for the Lost City of the Incas." He blew out a long breath and tried to gather his thoughts. "Gotta say Alex, none of this is filling me with confidence."

"There's more."

"Oh, happiness."

"I was reviewing the hotel's external CCTV and the three of these guys left together in a hired Jeep an hour or so ago, and they were joined by two other men."

"Who?"

"Can't help with the driver – he was already in the car when it pulled up at the hotel, but the other guy got out and they spoke for a moment. "His name's Ross Chastain, an American hired gun from Alabama. Former Delta soldier who was kicked out for insubordination and is now way past his prime. He was involved with

FARC via a drugs-running operation bringing coke into the US but he left them too."

"Kicked out of the Deltas, eh?" Hawke said, thinking aloud. "Maybe that explains why he turned, but why did he leave FARC?"

"Chastain and his men disagreed with the main movers and shakers at FARC headquarters when they declared their unilateral ceasefire back in 2015 and that's when he broke off and formed the Colombian Guerilla Force, or the CGF. So now he's all wrapped up with a FARC splinter group and it looks like he's hiring his men out to Saqqal and Kruger," Alex said. "These guys have trafficked coke to fund their terrorism since they started, and they use camps like this to train their men. They also have a good sideline in high-level kidnappings and ransoms."

"Is he what Americans call a douchebag?"

"Yup," Alex said. "Nailed it."

"Thanks. I have to say that this is not filling my day with sunshine and bluebirds."

"Mine either, but that's all I have. I wish I could help you more, but between my injuries and the whole Dad Thing it's impossible."

Only Alex Reeve could refer to her father's impending Presidency of the United States as the Dad Thing. Hawke knew in his heart she would have to stay in DC not only while she recovered from the attack on Elysium, but longer if she couldn't persuade her father that she could be safe from threats away from Secret Service protection, and that was going to be a tall order after Elysium. If she could be reached in that way on an isolated and heavily defended island then Jack Brooke was going to have a tough time letting her go anywhere else.

"And how is your dad?"

"Busier than usual, that's for sure. He keeps making jokes that the Electoral College is going to put Peterson in the White House instead of him and he can go back to Idaho, but it's just nerves."

"And how about you?" he asked, his voice quieter now. He expected an evasive response from her, as was her way, and that was exactly what he got.

"Just sitting in hospital hacking crap for you."

"I meant when you're out of hospital?"

A long pause. He heard the sound of a car horn outside her window and then a nurse said something to her before there was the sound of a door closing.

"Shit, I don't know, Joe! Everything's happening so fast. We were a team and then we got attacked and our base was smashed up, and now my Dad's the President-Elect and I'm in DC. What do you want me to say?"

"I'm sorry."

"Forget about it... listen – at first I wanted to tell Dad and his shadows to go screw themselves and that I had my own life to lead... that I was coming back to you guys, but now I think maybe this is a chance for us to build a bridge to each other, you know? Maybe the only chance."

"I understand."

"Listen, I'll look into these assholes more later."

"Thanks. We need to concentrate on the connection between them." he said, rubbing his temples. "Why are they working together?"

"That is for you to work out, Joe. We all have our problems. I have to decide whether to have chicken or beef for dinner tonight."

"A tough choice?"

"Not really. They both taste like plastic."

After he disconnected he waited in silence for a few moments, unsure how to break the news to the rest of the

40

team. As far as they were concerned, they were hunting Dirk Kruger, a corrupt archaeologist and part-time treasure hunter, with a view to stopping him getting to the Lost City. Now things had changed. A few simple words from Alex Reeve in Washington DC had changed the game completely. Why the hell would Dirk Kruger be associating with a Syrian terrorist rebel and a world-renowned expert in bacteria? He rubbed the back of his beck for a few seconds and sighed before getting up from his seat and walking to the others.

"And?" Lexi looked up expectantly.

"And we're in more shit than we thought," he said frankly.

"When were we ever in less shit than we thought?" Lea said.

"This is true…" Reaper said with a sympathetic nod of his head. "Always much more shit than you think… in life, I mean."

Scarlet yawned. "Spit it out, *darling*, and while you're at it, why not turn that frown upside down?" She punctuated the flippant comment by cracking the lid off a bottle of beer. He watched the low cabin lights of the jet illuminate the tiny cloud of condensed water vapor as it escaped from the neck of the bottle.

"Our South African friend has hooked up with a Syrian rebel of unknown affiliation and a bacteriologist."

"Shit," Scarlet said, pulling the beer away from her mouth before she had even taken a sip. "You'd better keep that shagging frown exactly where it is and tell me where I can get one."

"Quite, and I think this just about quadruples the pressure on us finding them before they get to whatever the hell they're looking for."

Reaper nodded and exhaled sharply. "Oui."

41

"Bottom line is, trying to stop Kruger finding the world's most famous lost city is one thing, but trying to stop known terrorists working alongside an expert with those sort of skills is quite another."

The tone he used was totally without his usual optimism, and he knew it. The pressure was on all right, and not just for the team to find Kruger and the Syrians. He had an extra pressure on his shoulders now, not only to lead these people into battle but to coordinate the whole operation as well. The heavy responsibility of this coupled with the recent loss of his friends and produced an almost unbearable burden, but he would die before he let his friends down.

*

Gagged and bound in the back of the Hyundai van, Ryan Bale felt himself turning inwards yet again. It always happened this way. No one understood him. Had anyone ever really loved him? Lea had left him. Sophie was taken from him.

At least he still had Maria.

But would he ever see her again? Kruger had played Russian roulette with him a few hours ago and he just didn't know if he was going to make it. In response, he had folded away into himself as if he were no more than an origami man, making sure the inside was hidden and nothing was exposed to the outside world. It always happened this way. No one understood him. He thought about his family back in London. His mother and father.

What were they doing now? If only he knew. Maybe they could help him, but he doubted it. His father's gambling and drinking had ended the relationship when he was still a teenager, and his mother... who knew where she was now? This was why he had ended up in an abandoned paint factory, launching DDOS attacks on American Government servers.

It always happened this way. No one understood him. They didn't know how noisy it was in his head sometimes. The thoughts fired through his brain like freight trains thundering through the night... they never stopped. He never forgot anything, and did people really know what that was like? Memories from twenty years ago fought for disk space with noun declensions and verb conjugations and the endless procession of historical facts and figures that rattled in his mind like old water pipes.

No one understood any of this. No one understood how noisy it was inside his head, and how Maria calmed it down. How her touch was a distraction sent from heaven. With her, he actually thought he could be normal and tune into the same frequency as his friends. If anything happened to her he knew any chance he might have of normality would be reduced to static, an uncontrollable white noise sending him inside himself over and over again.

Where's your spirit of adventure?

He could hear him say it.

But what would Hawke do in a situation like this? Grab the weird masked man at the wheel, knock him out... take his gun, kill the others and then slam open the rear doors and tumble to safety in the street? Ryan didn't have the strength or skills to fight his way through these men and he knew it would end in failure. He felt his spirit of adventure slowly evaporate and disappear into the ether.

Since Kruger had dragged him unconscious out of the ocean beneath the Oracle's Seastead his life had been a living hell. Kruger had kept him alive for his mind and what he could get out of it, but also as a bargaining chip with the ECHO team. How long this would continue he had no idea. He had been beaten and lived with the threat of murder every minute. All he could do to get through the torture was to cling to the hope of seeing Maria Kurikova again. He hadn't seen her since they'd split up on the Seastead, and he hated that she thought he was dead. Being back with her on the safety of Elysium was all that was keeping him going.

CHAPTER SEVEN

Bogotá

As soon as he saw it through the field glasses, Hawke saw Alex's research had been bang on the money. This was no full-scale FARC rebel camp. Those were ten times bigger than this and usually far away from the prying eyes of the cities. What he was looking at now was an impressive three storey mansion perched in the hills high above Bogotá – terracotta tiled roof, intricate white Colonial architecture and a neat balustrade running around the top floors.

It sat like a Puna hawk on a cliff-edge, overlooking a vast valley of feijoa trees and partially hidden behind the passionfruit vines twisting up its Roman arcades and double-hung windows. From their elevated position in the hills above the house, Hawke was able to see a good two acres of flattened ground in the property's west where some smaller chalets were situated and a jumble of other less impressive buildings. This must where Chastain's CGF training goes on, he thought.

Two Bell Kiowas were taking in some sunshine in the center of the training area. Normally used for direct-fire support, these were probably just used for transporting men and weapons through the mountains. The roads here were unsealed and the hairpin bends were very unforgiving if you made a mistake.

He watched small groups of men and a handful of women as they went about their business in the camp.

They would feel totally safe up here, and that was a sense of false security Hawke was going to exploit.

They seemed relaxed as they milled about, and now a man in a hard-worn sweat-stained Gambler hat strolled out of the mansion with his hands in his pockets and stood in the middle of the training area. He leaned forward and casually spat on the ground, and then removed his hat for a second to wipe the sweat from his forehead.

Beside him was the unmistakable figure of Dirk Kruger in his battered suede safari hat, black shirt and crocodile boots. A moment later two more men appeared in view – Hawke instantly recognized them from the Cartagena CCTV as Ziad Saqqal and Bashir Jawad. Chastain appeared to be showing them the training area and was pointing out the choppers and the contents of some plastic banana crates, but something told Hawke they weren't admiring bananas.

"They're our guys, all right," Hawke said, passing the field glasses to Reaper. "The whole Groovy Gang all together... but no sign of Ryan."

Reaper looked through the binoculars and gently nodded his head. "Oui – we know Kruger and the others all match Alex's description perfectly, but as you say – no Ryan."

Chastain yelled some orders and moments later a number of the men were running around the training area while holding their assault rifles above their heads. Another man was shouting at them in Spanish. Another group of men began loading the banana crates into the Kiowas.

"There goes the gear for the Inca mission," Hawke said. "I wonder what goodies a man like Chastain packs for a holiday to the Lost City?"

"Certainly not deodorant by the looks of his shirt," Scarlet said.

Lea sighed. "Guns, ammo, rappel lines, Maglites, glow sticks... you name it."

Hawke nodded. "I think you're on the money."

"They don't look too scary to me," Scarlet said.

"Don't get cocky. These are the men who have turned their backs on the peace settlement that FARC have committed to with the Colombian Government. I'm thinking they're not going to be a pushover."

Reaper watched through the field glasses as a small crew of men in the far corner of the training quad set up a machine gun.

"They've got an NSV to play with mes amis," he said, passing the binoculars back to Hawke.

"A what?" Luis said from the Jeep.

"It's an old Soviet heavy machine gun," Hawke said. "Eats up fifty-round boxes like a hungry wolf on a lamb. Replaced now by the Kord, but still a savage little beast. Eight hundred bullets per minute in our faces so try and stay out of its way everyone."

"Good advice," Reaper said with a calm nod of his head.

"Time for the off?" Lea said.

Hawke nodded and put the binoculars on the front seat. "Let's do it."

They told Luis to stay with the Jeep, and after tooling up with as many weapons as they could carry, they hiked straight down the old goat track and made their way toward Chastain's mansion. Hawke knew they would be outnumbered, but they had the element of surprise, plus he was willing to bet that aside from Chastain, the enemy would have zero Special Forces experience, and that gave them an edge.

Closer to the property now, they waited in the jungle while they made another surveillance of the enemy, counting guns and looking for any surprises. The only thing out of the ordinary was a large cage partially covered in vines which was situated a couple of hundred yards from the main house. It looked like it had some kind of viewing platform above it.

"What the hell is that?" Lea said, passing Hawke the binoculars.

He checked it out. "Looks like panthers to me... two of them."

"Why the hell are they in that cage?" Lexi asked.

"I dread to think," Scarlet said. "But I doubt Chastain keeps them for petting."

"We can worry about that later," the Englishman said. "Let's do this."

They fanned out and broke into two units. One led by Scarlet went to the south of the camp while Hawke's team dropped below the ridge line and approached from the north. Reaper kicked things off when he threw a grenade and took out several men hanging around one of the chalets, and then Scarlet followed suit by destroying one of the Jeeps with another grenade.

The reaction was furious, but panicked, and soon Chastain's men had split into two groups. One moved into the hills to the south of the property in pursuit of Scarlet while the other skirted the carnage of the burning chalets and moved toward Hawke's unit.

"Forward!" Hawke shouted.

Their guns blazed as they advanced toward the enemy, and Reaper felt a burst of morale as he watched the CGF men back at the mansion crumble and scatter. They were showing their weakness in the face of SBS, SAS and Foreign Legion training but there was no time for pride or premature celebrations.

Hawke had seen a group of men sprinting behind the Kiowas toward the NSV and that meant trouble for everyone. It was at the far western end of the training quad but it had a range of around one mile, which meant they were well in its sights. Not only that, but the sub-unit who had gone into the jungle south of the house had now regrouped and was starting to advance toward them from the west, creating a classic pincer movement. With the NSV on their right flank they would easily drive them into the loving arms of Chastain's team back in the cover of the mansion ahead of them.

Hawke's team doubled back and dipped below the ridge to the north of the training ground before coming in behind the sub-unit. Across the flattened grassy quad they watched a two-man crew open fire at Scarlet and the others, its vicious muzzle flashing white and orange as it spat out over a dozen rounds per second.

Hawke grabbed a grenade, pulled the pin out with his teeth and tossed it into the NSV nest and watched as the men reacted to it with savage, animal panic. They fumbled over each other for it, and then gave up and decided to flee, but it was too late. The explosion blasted them and the NSV to pieces and scattered the debris and body parts in a wide area around the nest.

"We need to get back to the others," Hawke said. "Chastain must have ordered an evacuation – the Kiowas are firing up."

"Not so fast, Joe..." Reaper raised his hand and pointed through a gap in the trees. Hawke looked through the gaps in between the trunks and saw the mansion. Standing in front of it was a smirking Ross Chastain and a huddle of men scanning the jungle with guns in their hands.

"Something's happening," Reaper said.

Hawke waved a mosquito away and stared at the men. "I don't believe it."

"What's going on?" Lea said, taking the field glasses.

"He's alive!" Hawke said.

Kruger gave an order and a moment later some men in jungle camos dragged Ryan out of the property and threw him down in the dirt.

"I don't believe it," Lea said. "I really thought he was dead. When I saw Kruger on the CCTV I thought maybe there was a chance, but even then..."

"Not me," Hawke said. "I knew he was alive."

The sight of Ryan Bale had lifted his spirits. What he had told the others about never giving up on him was true, but what he hadn't told them was how close he had come to deciding he was dead and letting him go.

And then Chastain called out into the trees. "All right, assholes... listen up! I don't know who the hell you are or what you want, but this guy's going to get it in the neck right now if y'all don't make like in the movies, and come out with your hands up. Any funny business and he's dead before your next breath."

CHAPTER EIGHT

Hawke clenched his jaw with rage and frustration, and knew he had no choice but to submit to Chastain's demands. Ryan was as good as dead if he defied him. Now, the former Delta was pushing his gun into the young man's temple.

"Drop your weapons everyone," Hawke said.

Hawke lowered his gun and stepped out of the jungle. He raised his hands above his head and walked slowly toward Chastain and the others. The rest of the team followed him. Across the other side of the training area he saw Scarlet drop her gun and follow his lead.

Chastain was close enough to see face to face now. Hawke studied the creases on his face, the blinking eyes and the lizard-like lick-of-the-lips and didn't like what he saw..

"Easy there, tiger," Chastain said, pulling a holstered Colt out from his side with surprising swiftness and raising it to the center of Hawke's face. "Hands up nice and high." His narrow eyes crawled over Reaper's tattoos. "That goes for you to, Foreign Legion. I don't know who the hell you are, but you certainly ain't like the kind of people who usually wind up here. Mr Corzo! Go and get their guns."

Carlos Corzo glanced at Chastain, flicked his cigarette into the air and walked over to the tree line where Hawke and the others had dropped their weapons. He returned a moment later and dumped them in a heap in front of Ross Chastain's boots.

"What have we here then?" He pushed the guns around with the steel toecap of his boot and nodded with appreciation. "A professional outfit."

Hawke knew he had done the right thing given the cards he had to play with at the time, but he was already regretting it. Then Chastain hit him hard in the face with the butt of the Colt and knocked him off his balance. He gasped in surprise and fell to the ground.

"No one comes on to my property and screws with me, you British asshole."

Hawke's head swam as he nearly lost consciousness. The pain of the pistol-whipping burned through his jaw and head, and his mouth filled with blood. He felt something moving around on his tongue, and realized Chastain had knocked one of his teeth out. He spat it at him in anger, and it left a bloody trail on his white shirt as it tumbled into the gravel at his feet.

Chastain raised his pistol to hit him again, but something made him stop. He gave an order and two of the men pulled Hawke to his feet and dragged him over to the others. "Who are you?"

"I'm the local health inspector," Hawke said. "Here to look for cockroaches."

"I said, what's your name, asshole?"

Hawke looked at Ryan. "Are you all right, mate?"

"I'm fine…"

"I want your name!" Chastain barked.

"I know his name," Kruger said. He stepped off the veranda and calmly placed a cigarette on his lip. Taking all the time in the world, he took a box of matches from his pocket and lit the cigarette. Blowing blue smoke into the muggy air he waved the match out and tossed it on the dirt. "It's Hawke – Joe Hawke. He and the rest of these bastards run an outfit called ECHO. They tried to kill me in the middle of the Atlantic. Very nasty bunch of bastards." He dragged on the cigarette and then turned to Lea, placing his fingers under her chin and raising her face up to his. "I was so very sad to read about Dickie Eden's misfortune."

Lea scowled at him. "Take your hands off me, you scum."

He nodded silently and then delivered a hefty backslap knocking her to the dirt. Hawke leaped forward to her defense but was attacked by two of Chastain's man. One hooked his foot out from under him while the other punched him hard in the back of the head, sending him crashing into the dusty gravel at their boots.

"Down boy!" Kruger yelled, and they all fell about laughing.

Except Saqqal who looked at his watch. "We need to get on."

Chastain spat on the bull grass as he strolled the short distance toward them. "You boys surely do know how to put on a show, but let me tell you that killing my men was a big mistake." As Hawke struggled up on all fours, Chastain kicked him hard in the ribs.

"Leave him alone, you coward!" Lea said, her lip still bleeding from Kruger's slap. She was now pinned against the iron trim of a fence with the muzzle of an assault rifle pointing in her face.

"Ziad is right," Chastain said. "We have better things to do than play with you assholes."

"Like play with your own arsehole, you mean?" Scarlet said.

"Shut up!" Chastain screamed, his calm composure cracking for a brief moment. He turned to Saqqal and spoke for a few moments. The Syrian nodded and then Chastain ordered a man into the house. He returned a few seconds later with someone who shocked them all.

Saqqal saw their horror and smiled. "Allow me to introduce Mr Rajavi."

A well-built man stepped off the veranda and into the Colombian sunshine. He was well over six feet tall and was so muscular he looked like he was built of bricks.

But his enormous muscles weren't what they were staring at.

Hawke fixed his eyes on the dead, expressionless face of the man as he walked closer and stood beside Saqqal. At first Hawke couldn't decide what was wrong with the man's face. It looked almost normal, and yet there was something not right about it that his instincts just wouldn't let go.

And then he worked it out. The man's face wasn't real, but a mask of a human face. A silicon mask that was so close to reality one glance wasn't enough to work it out, especially from a distance, but a longer look, up-close, and the deception was unveiled.

Saqqal noted their expressions and smirked with a demented pride as if he were displaying a rare animal.

"Mr Rajavi was mauled terribly by a Persian leopard while he was hunting them in the Zagros Mountains. He lost nearly all of his face, and let's just say the surgical reconstruction was not of the highest quality. Today he hides the horror behind this silicon mask, which apparently is a facsimile of the face he used to have before the attack. Excuse his reluctance to speak – he's not being rude. The sad truth is the leopard took his tongue along with everything else."

Rajavi's dark eyes blinked behind the mask, and the sound of his breathing grew in volume. The silicon mask was almost lifelike, but not quite, and that is what made is so creepy and unnerving. There was no way for any emotion to appear on the mask, so reading the mood behind the silicon was impossible, and yet the eyes were real, staring out at them all from behind the grotesque artifice of the shield he had erected between his disfigured face and the rest of the world.

"He's not being vain, you understand," Saqqal said. "The attack was savage, and the mask is there for your benefit, not his."

Chastain looked suspiciously at the man for a few moments. Hawke didn't know how long he had known Rajavi but it obviously wasn't enough to get used to the mask.

After a few long seconds, Chastain took a step back and moved closer to Lexi and brushed his hand over her breasts. "They are so beautiful," he whispered. "It's just such a shame to keep them locked up like this." He ripped her top open and exposed her underwear, making her flinch in disgust.

Hawke leaped forward to help her, but one of the men raised his rifle and struck him hard once again on the back of his skull, but this time with the heavy polymer butt of the weapon. Once again, Hawke fell to his knees in agony, desperately clinging to consciousness.

"All right," Kruger said. "Enough of this. We have work to do. I don't care how you get rid of this scum but do it now and then we can get out of here."

Chastain looked at the South African long and hard for a moment. He looked like he wanted to shoot him, but instead he ordered Corzo and Rajavi to take the ECHO team over to the cage.

The former Delta man strolled along beside them with his hands in his pockets and a grin on his face. "Let me introduce you to Bonnie and Clyde." They stepped through the tunnel of vines and got their first unobscured view of the cage. Hawke had been right – behind the bars two large black panthers were snoozing in different corners. The sides of the cage were at least ten feet high, but there was no roof on it.

"You're looking at two of the finest examples of *panthera pardus*, or to bozos like you, black jaguars."

"*Panthera onca*, you complete fool," Ryan said. "*Panthera pardus* is the black leopard."

Chastain stared at him. "Is that right?"

"It is."

Chastain gave Ryan a slap with the back of his hand and nearly knocked him over.

The young man's eyes burned with hatred as he wiped the blood from his mouth and Chastain laughed at his work. "As you can see, their little home is divided into two spacious rooms. The first cage is where they like to sleep and pass the day under the shade of the vines."

It was now that Hawke saw a dividing wall of bars running down the middle of the cage. "And what's this half for?"

Chastain grinned again. "Think of this end of the cage as their dining room... Corzo! That one right there is lunch." He pointed to Lea, and the Colombian marched over to her and grabbed her roughly by the arm.

Lea struggled against him as he dragged her across the scrubby grass and up to the viewing platform. Chastain laughed and spat on the grass. Pulled his pants up with one hand. Sniffed hard and turned to Hawke. "See, *boy*... the pleasure here is guessing which one of them cats is gonna get her first. They ain't been fed nothin' for four days... makes 'em keener."

Lea stared at the big cats, terrified as they awoke and began to pace around below her. "Joe!"

"*Joe!*" Chastain said in mockery. "*Save me!*" He laughed and joined them on the viewing platform for a better of the view. "No one gonna save you, darlin'."

But then it all changed.

The explosion was enormous, and rocked the ground they stood on. Behind them, the top floor of the mansion was now ablaze, and smoke was pouring from a large hole in the terracotta roof.

Chastain and Corzo turned to see Kruger and the Syrians scrambling away from the house and covering their heads from the debris that was now dropping from the sky. Saqqal looked rattled and immediately ordered his men into the nearest Kiowa. Kruger measured the situation and decided to flee with them.

It was all kicking off again.

CHAPTER NINE

Chastain staggered back along roof, his arms flailing as he went and a look of unbridled terror on his fat face. He tried to stop himself going over by clawing at the air. It was pointless, but he was driven by instinct to survive.

"What the hell was that?" Lea screamed.

"Luis!" Hawke yelled. He pointed to Luis who was on the rise halfway between the mansion and the Jeep. He was waving one of the grenade launchers in his hand.

"Well bugger me," Scarlet said, impressed.

"National Service!" the young Colombian called back.

But then they heard a scream and turned to see Chastain go over the edge and fall inside the panthers' enclosure. He landed in what he had smugly described as the dining room.

"Please...!" he screamed. " Oh, Jesus H. Christ, help me!"

"Call me crazy," Lea said coolly from the viewing platform, "but I don't think he can hear ya."

Clyde moved first, rising to all fours on his powerful haunches and turning his broad, square face toward the new arrival.

Chastain stumbled back a few yards to the edge of the cage, almost surprised when he walked into it. "Please... you can't do this to me."

"I thought you said it was fun?" Lea said.

Bonnie now got up and joined Clyde.

Chastain raised his head and saw his own chopper slowly rising above the training area, with Kruger,

Saqqal, Jawad and Rajavi all safely on board. He waved a fist in the air and screamed. "You bastard, Saqqal!"

"Looks like you need to learn how to make better friends," Hawke said, strolling over to join Lea as she climbed down from the platform.

Clyde growled, and began to pace up and down in front of Chastain. It was a low, deep growl that they all felt as much as heard.

"He sounds hungry," Lexi said. "When was the last time you fed them again?"

"I think he said four days ago," Reaper said.

"Ouch," Scarlet said. "Poor little kitty cats..."

The black panthers were now getting agitated.

"Did you know," Ryan said at last, "that all black panthers in Asia are leopards, but all black panthers in South America are jaguars?"

"I did not know that, mate," Hawke said. Ryan's voice was harder now, without the levity. Hawke thought he sounded ten years older than the last time he had heard him speak.

"Neither did I," Scarlet said. "Good to have you back, Ryan."

"Thanks."

"Yes, I damn well knew that!" Chastain said. His voice was now a desperate whisper as he sought to calm the angry panthers a few feet from him. "Just please get me the fuck outta here and you can have whatever you want, I swear!"

"We can have whatever we want already, darling," Scarlet said.

"C'est vrai," Reaper added, rolling a cigarette. His eyes were fixed on the thin line of tobacco in the folded paper, but he could hear and smell the panthers as they closed in on the former Delta soldier. All that was between him and the wild animals now was the partition gate.

"They are so beautiful," Lexi said. "It's just such a shame to keep them locked up like this."

She threw the lever and the partition gate began to creak open.

"You can't do this to me!" he shouted.

Hawke scanned the area and saw Corzo sprinting across the training area toward the Kiowa. Kruger made no effort to stop for him, but he got there all the same, leaping for his life and slamming into the portside skid. As the chopper ascended above the jungle canopy and disappeared into the west, Carlos Corzo was still dangling off the skid and hanging on for all he was worth.

"Hope the bastard falls off," Lea said, and then she heard a deep growl a few feet behind her. She turned to see Bonnie and Clyde crawling under the gap in the dividing bars and approaching Ross Chastain with hunger in their eyes.

"Please!" Chastain said, pleading with them one last time. "Let me out."

"Goodbye, Chastain," Lexi said, and slammed the vine-covered gate behind her as she left the cage area. As a horrendous mix of human screams and jaguar roars drifted above the vines, Lexi dusted her hands off and faced the others. "Don't go in there. It's a clawful mess."

"Oh, *please*," Scarlet said, rolling her eyes, but Hawke laughed.

"Love it."

Lea was still shaking as Hawke put his arms around her and held her tight. She liked the way it felt when he held her close. She felt safe, and for just a moment it was okay to let her guard down... the guard she had kept up since her father was taken from her. The buzzing wasp of hatred and regret that was behind every thought she ever had.

When she was in Joe Hawke's arms the wasp went away and she could breathe again. She was no fool. She had seen the way he'd looked at Maria Kurikova, and she had an idea there might be trouble with Alex Reeve on the horizon, but what else could she do?

She knew no one else in the world and all she'd ever wanted was peace and happiness. For a time, Richard Eden had offered it to her, but now even that looked like it was about to be taken away. Life was a hurricane, and Joe Hawke was her storm shelter. Solid, reliable, and always ready to take her in. Now, just seconds after almost being turned into cat food by Ross Chastain, she was so grateful to be alive she saw things with a renewed clarity.

"Come on you lazy bastards," Scarlet said. "Kruger's getting away." She flicked her cigarette into the bull grass and walked over to their weapons. "And we all owe Luis a beer."

CHAPTER TEN

They grabbed their weapons from the pile Corzo had made after their surrender and began to trudge back up the hill. The humidity was hell, and all around them the scream of the crickets and tree frogs rose up on both sides of the goat track as they got closer to the Jeep.

Halfway up, they found a smiling Luis Montoya with an old grenade launcher on his lap, and they introduced him to Ryan.

"Luis, meet Ryan Bale," Scarlet said. "Ryan, meet Colombian Ryan."

After the handshake, the attention turned from Luis's grenade intervention to Ryan Bale, newly rescued from the clutches of Dirk Kruger and Ziad Saqqal. When they were back at the Jeep and away from the burning mansion, Lea turned to him, kissed him on the forehead and looked him in the eye. "So what the hell happened?"

He looked dazed but pleased to be safe at last. "It's all a blur…" he said, peering over their heads and into the Jeep.

"He jumped off the scaffolding to stop Kruger, is what happened," Reaper said. "He's a hero."

Ryan blushed. "But after *that* it's a blur. I thought – this guy's an archaeologist, how hard can he be? We fought on the deck and I realized Korać was trying to blow up the petrol tank. That was when I broke away from Kruger and tried to jump off the boat. I was in the air when the bullets hit the tank and sparked the petrol. There was an enormous explosion that sent me flying like Superman…"

"In your dreams," Scarlet said.

"All right, like a *bird*, and the next thing I know Dirk Kruger was dragging me out of the water and smacking my face to bring me around." He looked in the Jeep again. "Where's Maria?"

"But I searched the area," Reaper said.

Lea looked at him and bit her lip. "And we searched it again when we left in the boat." Her voice was growing quieter.

"That's because he took me into one of the sailing boats on the south jetty and tied me up at gunpoint. I watched you sail away from the porthole. It was a tough moment. I thought he was going to kill me."

Lea felt a wave of hatred for Kruger rise in her soul, only to be pushed out of the way by a stronger feeling of sadness for what Ryan had been put through, and what he now had to be told. "And then what?"

"Then we sailed to the Azores where some of his associates arranged a private flight to Lisbon. Is Maria on Elysium?"

"And then to Cape Town?" Lexi asked.

Ryan shook his head. "No. That's what I was expecting but when we got to Lisbon he made contact with people in South Africa who told him about the Syrians. He and Saqqal wanted to meet to discuss the Lost City so a meeting was arranged in Tunis."

"Tunis?" Hawke said.

Ryan nodded. "We were there less than a day. It was decided that Kruger would secure the Mask of Inti while Saqqal arranged the extra muscle with Chastain. I don't know what Saqqal is looking for but it's not any lost treasure. He kept going on about Utopia."

Hawke frowned. "Utopia?"

"Uh-huh, but no idea what that means. I think he's a few clowns short of circus, if you ask me."

"So what happened next?" Lexi asked.

"Then the plan was to meet up in Colombia, and that's where you entered the picture." He sighed heavily. "Which is good, because Kruger said he was only keeping me alive until he had no further use for my skills... and then the plan was to shoot me... I'm so glad it's over. Now, would someone please tell me where Maria is?"

"Come with me, Ryan," Reaper said. "We need to talk."

"About what?"

"Please..."

Reaper flicked his roll-up away and put his tattooed arm on Ryan's shoulder as he wheeled him away from the group. They walked back along the track a few yards and the Frenchman began talking quietly.

Lea watched the conversation from a distance, her heart breaking as she watched Ryan get smashed yet again with the terrible news about Maria Kurikova and how she was killed by Ekel Kvashnin back on the Seastead. The young man walked around in circles for a moment, with his head in his hands and then collapsed to the floor as he broke down. Reaper tried to comfort him with a heavy hand but Ryan pushed him away and then staggered to his feet before scrambling into the jungle.

Reaper returned slowly to the group and began to roll another cigarette. "I told him what happened. I told him she was a hero."

"He needs time," Lea said, anxiously scanning the tree line for any sign of her ex-husband.

"That can't have been easy to take," Hawke said flatly, working hard to keep any emotion out of his voice. "Not after Sophie."

Scarlet sighed. "No..."

*

The journey into Bogotá was winding, stuffy and silent. Ryan sat in the back and stared wordlessly out the window as the jungle slowly turned into the suburbs of the city. When they got back to the hotel they bought beers and moved away from the bar to talk. Ryan pulled a piece of grubby paper from his pocket, handed it to Luis, and after downing his drink he turned and walked right back to the bar on his own.

"I need another drink."

"What's this?" Lea said.

Without turning or stopping, Ryan called out over his shoulder. "The marks on the mask Kruger nicked from Cartagena."

Luis Montoya's eyes widened like two full moons when he saw the sketches Ryan had made from his memory of the Mask of Inti. "This is incredible... are you sure it is what you saw?" He looked up but saw Ryan was now at the bar and making his order.

"Can you help us, Luis?" Lexi said.

"Maybe."

Scarlet sighed. "Helpful. Kruger's got the mask and is presumably well on his way and we're buggering around with a maybe."

"Easy, Cairo," Hawke said, raising his hand to calm her. "He's doing his best and he's all we've got. I don't think Ryan's with us at the moment." Looking into the bar he saw Ryan downing his third consecutive whisky.

"Yeah, I noticed that," she said.

Lea stepped into the fray. "What's that supposed to mean?"

"Stand down, kitten," Scarlet said. "It's supposed to mean precisely nothing."

"I can help, I think," Luis said, ignoring the obvious tension in the room. "But these are very unusual symbols. I can see why Héctor hid it away."

"Tell us what you can," Reaper said, lighting a cigarette and moving over to the window.

Hawke passed a tense hand over his face and sighed before crashing down on a soft chair. "Yes – please, Luis. Anything you have could help us."

"If these sketches are accurate then they are Incan in origin, which is not surprising, but they're not entirely consistent with the traditional Incan style."

"What are you saying?" Lexi asked.

"I'm not sure I can read them – at least not this one here. It's very confusing. It appears to be Indian in origin."

"As in curries?" Scarlet said.

"As in the Hindu Mandala," Luis said. "Are you sure Ryan can't help?"

Lea looked over at Ryan. He was slumped over the bar and leaning into a good-looking woman with a low-cut top and lots of lipstick. "I think Ryan's still MIA."

Luis looked confused. "MIA?"

"Missing in Action."

"Ah… I see. What about this Alex?"

"She's been called away to be with her family," Hawke said, and didn't elaborate. "We can communicate with her but it's on her schedule not ours."

Reaper stubbed out his roll-up and stepped over to them, stopping to clap his heavy hand on Luis's shoulder. "What they're saying, mon ami, is that it's all down to *you*." And with that he raised his lager and took a long drink before sighing with satisfaction.

"So speak up or forever hold your peace," Scarlet said.

"I don't think I can help you. I am concerned by the presence of the Hindu Mandala on this mask. It should not be here. I can only presume it has been added later as a joke."

"I wouldn't bank on it," Lexi said.

"What do you mean?"

"She means we've found many archaeological pieces which don't exactly add up to make sense," Hawke said. "What we need to focus on right now is what these markings mean. Kruger has killed people for the mask and he obviously knows what it means. That means we have to know as well or we can't stop him."

"Yes!" Luis said, leaping up from his seat and pacing up and down. "I agree, but what?" In his hand he was still holding the folded paper Ryan had drawn on, and as he raised it to his eyes for a closer look he knocked Reaper's beer off the table where it tumbled to the floor and spilled out all over the carpet.

"Oh, sorry!"

"De rien," Reaper said, and grabbed another beer from the bar while Luis hurriedly mopped up the mess on the floor with a napkin.

"What were you going to say, Luis?" Lea said, concealing the frustration in her voice.

"I think we're going to need to show this to Mauricio Balta."

"Who's he?" Scarlet said.

"He's the curator of the Larco Museum in Lima."

"Lima, Peru?" Lea said.

Luis looked at her. "Is there another one?"

CHAPTER ELEVEN

Lima

Their flight to the Peruvian capital was uneventful and boring and as soon they had cleared customs they were piling into a hired SUV and racing into the city. Lea watched the suburbs rush past in a blur as Hawke weaved the Pajero deftly in and out of the lanes on the highway, and her mind drifted to Dirk Kruger and his new friends, Saqqal and Jawad. As for Rajavi, the Iranian strongman, she shuddered to think what was behind the mask.

She hated that she didn't know what Kruger was up to. Was he now using his massive wealth and grubby black market connections to expand his network in a bid to beat them to the truth they had sought for so long? Even worse was the fact that now they had two enemies to fight – the Oracle and his mysterious Athanatoi and now Kruger and his nutcase Syrian terrorist friends and their weird obsession with Utopia – whatever the hell that was.

She glanced in the mirror and looked at Ryan. He was sullenly staring out of the window but his eyes were covered by a pair of sunglasses. He'd pulled his messy hair forward to hide his face. He hadn't spoken since Reaper told him about Maria's death and she knew he was turning inside himself again. This time it would be worse than ever. The anger and misery of grief was whispering its poison in his mind and only time could heal that.

"We're here," Hawke said, interrupting her thoughts. She looked up to see they were in the rear car park of a coffee shop in the Miraflores district of the city. They had called ahead to the Larco Museum and Balta had told them he wanted to meet here. She unbuckled her seatbelt and climbed down from the chunky SUV before following Hawke, Scarlet and Luis into the coffee shop. Reaper and Lexi stayed in the Pajero with a silent Ryan Bale.

Out the front window of the coffee shop they saw huge crowds of people jostling for space along the street.

"What the hell is going on?" Hawke asked.

"Lollapalooza," Scarlet said matter-of-factly. "Good line-up this year as well."

"Like who?" asked Lea.

"Foo Fighters, Aerosmith, Chili Peppers, Temper Trap, Kaiser Chiefs, Chainsmokers..."

"An excellent line-up," Hawke said, giving them a look. "I'm especially proud of the fact I only recognized about two bands out of that lot."

Lea rolled her eyes and took a step toward their guide. "Do you see him, Luis?"

Luis Montoya stood on his tiptoes to peer over the heads of the customers in the busy shop and looked down-hearted for a few moments before a smile suddenly flashed on his face. "There! He's over by the other window."

Lea followed his gaze and saw Professor Mauricio Balta innocuously stirring some sugar into a large cup of coffee. The two empty cups on his table told her he'd been waiting for some time.

They approached him, Hawke scanning the small space for anything suspicious as they went, and as their shadows fell over his table, Balta looked up from his coffee and smiled at them. "You must be here about the mask?"

Hawke held out his hand. "That's right, Doc. The name's Hawke, and this is Lea Donovan, Scarlet Sloane and Doctor Luis Montoya from the University of Bogotá."

The legs of his chair scratched on the tiled floor as he pushed it back to greet them, meticulously shaking their hands with a polite bow of the head. "Please, take a seat," he said, gesturing at the empty chairs he had obviously arranged around his little table.

"Thanks," Lea said and sat down opposite him. The others joined her.

Balta spoke first. "So, is it true? Does the Mask of Inti really exist?"

Luis nodded his head. "It most certainly does, Professor Balta! Héctor Barrera saw it with his own eyes... He *held* it in his hands."

"Our friend saw it too," Lea said. "And he has an unusually powerful eidetic memory. He can recall everything he sees for days afterwards. That is how he was able to draw this."

Hawke pulled out the paper from the inside pocket of his jacket, unfolded it and flattened it on the table before sliding it across to Balta.

Balta opened his eyes wide and gasped with surprise. "Are you telling me that your friend really saw *this* on the Mask of Inti?"

"Yes," Lea said. "But now we're out of ideas. That's why we need your help."

"This is truly remarkable," he said, unable to take his eyes off the slip of paper. Finally he raised his head and stared at Lea. "Are you absolutely certain this is what was on the mask?"

Lea nodded enthusiastically. "Absolutely."

"What's so special about it, professor?" Hawke said.

"What's so special about it?" he asked, raising his eyes to meet them all. "If this is real then we must get back to my office at once. If this isn't a joke, then what you have here is the key to locating the Lost City of the Incas."

CHAPTER TWELVE

Hawke scanned the corridor while Balta fumbled for his keys and opened his door. His office was a modest state of affairs in the Larco Museum in the Pueblo Lire district and moments later they were all gathered inside while their host shuffled into an adjoining room to fetch his life's work.

"So what's all the fuss about then?" Scarlet said, looking down her nose at the furniture.

Balta called out in response from the next room. "These markings are certainly Inca pictographs, although greatly simplified, presumably due to the restricted space on the mask."

"What do they say?" Lexi asked. Reaper stood behind her silently rolling a cigarette and watching the street outside. Balta shuffled back into the room and scratched his head as he scanned the office for something.

"The pictographs are simply depictions of Inti and the sun, but it's the last one that has my interest. That's why I wanted to come back to my work." He stopped speaking and began furiously searching through a box file on his desk.

"So what's the big surprise?" Hawke asked, looking once again at Ryan's hand-drawn sketch.

"The final pictograph on the mask is a crude depiction of the Mandala."

"That's what I thought," Luis said. "But I really think we must be mistaken."

"But what does that mean?" Lexi asked.

Balta looked at her. "The Mandala is a religious symbol which represents our universe."

"I'm not convinced," Luis said, looking doubtful. "It doesn't look all that much like a Mandala, not to mention the fact the Mandala is from India. The more I look at it the less I think it's a Mandala."

"You mentioned India before," Hawke said. "What the hell is an Indian symbol doing on an Inca mask?"

Luis shook his head and put his hands in his pockets. "Quite. Are you *certain*, professor?"

"I am certain, young man," Balta said without hesitation. "And I am perfectly aware that the Mandala's provenance is from the Indian religions. I am also aware that it is to be found here on this satellite image." With these words Balta swung a piece of paper out of the box file and held it up in front of the team.

"Woah!" Lea said. "That's the same damned thing, isn't it?"

Balta nodded. "Yes, but the one you see on this paper is much more complex. The rendering on the mask is clearly a simplified version."

Hawke stepped forward and looked at the image on the paper in Balta's hands. "So where does this one come from?"

Luis Montoya sighed. "It's one of the Nazca Lines hidden up in the mountains just east of the more famous geoglyphs on the plain. Conspiracy theorists claim it's an Indian Mandala but I have never bought into it."

"You cannot deny the similarity!" Balta said, raising his voice.

"They do look almost identical," Lexi said.

"And their similarity to the Indian Mandala is almost exact."

"Almost," Luis said with another sigh. "But not exact."

Balta shook his head. "How can you say that? The Indian Mandala is clear enough for anyone to see, and right here in the mountains of Peru there is one carved into the rock that is almost identical in its nature."

Luis looked unpersuaded, but Hawke could see the similarity when Lea showed him the pictures of an Indian Mandala she had found on her phone. "I don't know," the Englishman said. "If they're not connected in any way then that's one hell of a coincidence."

"Exactly my point!" exclaimed Balta. "The Mandala geoglyph at the Nazca Lines site is what we have called the Sun-Star and Cross. It is one of the most famous of all the glyphs – over one hundred meters in length!"

Luis gave him a look of pity. "Most famous among crazy conspiracy theorists, maybe."

Balta dismissed Luis's objections with a wave of his hand. "The Sun-Star and Cross glyph is one of the most precise pieces of geometry in the ancient world, and yet we still don't know exactly what it represents. Many believe it is a celestial map charting some universal space we don't even know about yet!"

"How did the people who carved it into the mountain get so much geometric precision over a thousand years ago?" Lea asked.

Balta shrugged and smiled. "I don't know, but this is why I do what I do!"

With Balta's enthusiastic words still hanging in the air of his office, Hawke looked down at the satellite photograph of the Sun-Star and Cross, sitting innocuously in the Peruvian mountains. He saw what Balta was describing easily enough – the design of the Sun-Star itself did seem to match the pictures he had just seen of the Hindu Mandala, but the professor wasn't finished yet.

"More intriguing than that are these symbols here," he said. "When I mentioned this back at the café I never dreamed it could be real, but after consulting my papers... I can hardly believe I'm saying this but they really do appear to be giving us some sort of clue about..."

"About what?"

"About... *Paititi*."

"And what's that again?" Scarlet said. "Didn't Lund mention something about that?"

Ryan sighed and collapsed in a leather chair in the corner.

"Paititi," Luis said, once again with a sigh, "is supposed to be the famous Lost City of the Incas."

"There is no supposed about it," snapped Balta. "There is ample evidence for its existence, and men have tried to locate it dozens of times – never with any success, I might add. But now the Lost City of Gold may be within our reach! For generations man has sought the incredible treasures within its hallowed ruins but never have they had anything like this to help them locate it!"

"I don't know. How do we even know it exists?" Lea asked. "I mean, *really?*"

Balta smiled at her, barely able to contain his excitement. "Inca legends are very clear in their description of the Lost City. They describe it as being somewhere north of Cusco and to the east of the Andes."

"But a legend is a legend," Lexi said, unpersuaded.

Balta paced up and down his office, his excitement growing. "Then think about the massive gold that the Spanish plundered from Cusco. We know from Inca descriptions that they only got their hands on the smallest fraction of the full amount of their treasure – so where is the rest? Why, in the Lost City, of course!"

"So you say..." Luis said.

"I do say! And if all that is not enough – what about the Mask of Inti? We now know it exists because your friend saw it for a few precious moments. That mask was found on board the San José, a Spanish galleon that was obviously carrying looted Inca gold back to Spain! If your friend's sketch of the mask is accurate, then the piece of paper it's on is worth a thousand times more than everything found on that raised galleon!"

"How so?" Lea asked. "It's just one mask."

"Oh *God...*" Ryan mumbled.

"Because of the clues carved into it!"

Hawke sighed. "All right, prof. I think you'd better walk us through these symbols in a little more detail."

"It's very straight-forward – these smaller pictograms here say *Follow the Sun, Cross and Sacred Stone and The Tomb of Pachacuti will illuminate the Path to Paititi.*"

"That's pretty unambiguous, I admit," Hawke said.

"To me," Balta continued, "this says quite clearly that the road to Paititi will start in the tomb of Pachacuti."

Lea spoke next. "So the next question is obviously who's that and where's his body?"

Balta looked at her and shook his head with confusion. "Pachacuti, or in full, Pachacuti Inca Yupanqui was the ninth Sapa Inca."

"Oh," Scarlet said. "That clears it up then."

"Like a king or something?" Lea asked.

"In a way, yes, but more than that. The Sapa Inca was also known as the Apu, which is loosely translated as the Divinity. Pachacuti was the ninth such man, and most archaeologists today believe it was he who ordered the construction of Machu Picchu as his royal estate."

"Machu Picchu?" Hawke said.

"Yes, the famous Inca citadel in the Urubamba mountains."

76

"And is his tomb there?"

Balta looked confused and shook his head. "There have always been differing accounts about the location of Pachacuti's final resting place, but recently discovered documents from the Sixteenth Century suggest he was buried in Toqocachi, which was the Imperial City of the Incas in present-day San Blas."

"So what you're saying is we don't know where his tomb is?"

"Yes, up until today, but now this sketch might have changed all that."

"I admit it's pretty interesting," Scarlet said. "For once."

"If you think this is interesting now, wait until I tell you about this symbol here." As he spoke he indicated the penultimate symbol – a small stepped cross with twelve points around on its outer edge and a circle in the center.

"A weird cross thing with scratches in the middle of it?" Lea said.

Balta looked up at her. "It's not a weird cross, but a chakana, or the Andean cross. It represents a simplified compass, and the scratches are not scratches, my dear."

"Then what are they?"

"They are a rendering of what the Inca called talking knots, or quipus."

"Come again, doc," Scarlet said.

He looked at her, confused.

Lea rolled her eyes. "She means please explain further, Professor Balta."

"Ah…"

"I read about those once," Lexi said. "Aren't they the Inca system of measuring distances and time and whatever?"

"The term you're struggling to find is Inca *metronomy*," Ryan said.

"The man is right," Balta said.

"And what do these quipus tell us, professor?" Lea asked.

"The markings are for Fifty Tupus, and then Fifty Rikras."

"What's fifty tupus?" Hawke asked.

"A hell of a lot messier than twenty-two poos, I'd think," Scarlet said.

"Give it a rest, Cairo," Lea said. "We're trying to do serious business."

Scarlet grinned at her. "Fifty Tupus sounds like serious business to me."

"The *tupu*," Balta continued with an admonishing glance at Scarlet, "is an Incan unit of distance, measuring about six kilometers. I think we're being told to follow the sun and cross if we want to find Pachacuti's tomb, and from there he will lead us to the Lost City of Paititi."

"At this Toqocachi place?" Lea asked.

"Maybe," Balta said. "We'll need to get a map."

Hawke turned to face Balta. "I'm concerned the people who stole the mask may come for you next, professor, so we need to hurry. Get Google Earth fired up, Lea."

"Wait."

It was Reaper's voice. He was still watching out the window but now he was pulling his gun from his belt. "I think maybe a little trouble is coming our way."

CHAPTER THIRTEEN

"Stay away from the windows," Hawke said to Balta, and moved to join Reaper at the front. Before he had gone two paces Balta's entire office rocked with the force of a prodigious explosion from somewhere in the corridor.

"Double envelopment!" Scarlet yelled as the force threw her to the floor.

"Or pincer movement as we say in English," Lea said.

"That would have so much more authority," Scarlet said, shielding her head from the blast, "if only you could actually speak English, darling."

With plaster dust and wood splinters raining down from the explosion, they staggered to their feet and readied for a fight.

"I think they might have some grenades, ladies," Lexi said.

Hawke thought that was a good guess, but his concerns they would use a second grenade were put to bed when he heard men bundling into the building from the rear and approaching the professor's office door. More of the CGF rebels were now approaching the front of the office from the street.

Balta looked up with an expression of strained fear on his wrinkled face. "Are these the people you said would come for me?"

"Unless you forget to pay your council tax bill this month, then yes," Scarlet said.

"Will they kill me?"

"Only when they've used you."

Hawke took control. "Reaper and Scarlet take the back and Lea, Ryan and I will take the front. Lexi, you take Luis and the professor into the adjoining office. They want Balta but they might settle for Luis."

"Thanks," Luis said.

And with that the assault began.

"Flashbang!" Hawke yelled but the fuse was short and the next second it had detonated in a blinding flash of light and noise, and now in the dusty confusion created by the blast they were totally disoriented.

Lea staggered to her feet, coughing up plaster dust and trying to regain her balance. She was dimly aware of screaming but her head felt like it was wrapped in cotton wool. And then she saw the rebels as they burst into the office and fought their way toward Balta. They had the mask but they still needed the knowledge. In the confusion and chaos of the fight, Lea thought it was good to know that Dirk Kruger didn't know everything.

A rebel rushed her and took a swing, but she dodged it and ducked her head to avoid his follow-up punch. She grabbed his shoulders and kneed him hard in the groin. It was a dirty trick but he looked like he deserved it and she would use anything in her arsenal to defend herself. He doubled over and she thrust her right hand forward, striking his chin with a palm strike and knocking his head back. He toppled over on his arse and she finished the job with a swift kick, delivering her left boot around the right side of his chops and putting him to sleep for hours.

"Nighty night!" she said.

Across the room Ryan Bale was fighting with another man, but this time he looked like he meant it. She moved to help him but then she saw something had changed with her ex-husband. Usually he looked like he wanted to do anything but fight, but not this time. This time he was almost enjoying it as he pounded his fists on his opponent and sent him staggering back to get his balance back.

The fight had dragged Hawke into the corridor, and now he was grappling with another of the rebels and putting him in a choke hold. He grabbed his neck and squeezed hard, pushing his fingers behind his Adam's apple to finish the choke. The man's face went purple and he stopped breathing, but Hawke couldn't stop. At that second all he could think about was Maria Kurikova, and that heart-melting smile of hers. The fact she had walked way from her homeland to fight alongside him. The smell of her perfume. Ryan's loss... And the rage rose in him like molten lava as he faced an enemy so close to the one who had taken her life.

The man was unconscious now, but instead of letting him fall to the floor, Hawke pulled his arm back and powered a mighty fist into his face and smashed his nose to a pulp, and again and then again, and then...

"Joe! Leave it."

He turned to see Lea. She looked horrified at what he was doing. He wanted to scream, but instead he let the man's unconscious body fall to the floor and sprinted back into the office and the main fight, pumped full of adrenalin. Back in the fray, he saw the surprising sight of Ryan Bale taking out his frustrations on one of the rebels.

Ryan was not a born fighter – it wasn't in his nature – but he was a tall man, nearly as tall as Hawke, and if he put on some weight and changed his attitude he knew he could be dangerous. Today, it looked like something in him had snapped and it didn't take a genius to know what. Either way, it seemed to Hawke that perhaps Ryan Bale was a different man now, and that just maybe he had taken his first steps toward pointing his life in a new direction.

Hawke noticed any rebels who were still standing began to retreat and leave the fight, fleeing from the office, all except the man who was fighting Ryan.

The young Londoner moved into the fight now instead of backing away, and continued to deliver a salvo of blows into the man's face. Blood was pouring down from his opponent's broken nose, and he was spitting it out of his mouth as he tried to fight back but if Ryan had learned anything from Joe Hawke it was never give your enemy a chance to get back on his feet.

If he was going down, then send him down.

And then he did something that stunned them all.

He rammed a powerful head-butt into the goon's face and knocked him out cold.

"Holy Shit, Ry!"

But Ryan didn't stop there, and padded forward to the unconscious man. He grabbed his collar and punched him again, and then thundered a kick into his side.

Lea ran to him and pulled him back. "Ryan! He's out cold, leave it!"

"He killed Maria!" Ryan screamed.

"No... he didn't."

"Yes, he did! And he killed Sophie too! They're all the same."

Another kick.

Hawke stepped over and pushed Ryan away from the man. "Lea's right, mate. He's out cold. You won. And he's not the man who killed Maria. That was Ekel Kvashnin and he's fish food. Reap killed him on the Seastead."

Ryan was breathing hard, almost hyperventilating. Lea watched his chest heaving up and down and the blood pumping hard in the veins on his neck. "I'm sorry... you're right, of course."

"It's okay, mate," Hawke said. "You had to get it out somewhere." He glanced at the knocked-out man on the floor. "I guess that toerag was as good a place as anywhere."

"But it won't bring her back," Lea said gently, holding his shoulders and looking into his eyes. She was trying to find the old Ryan, the nerd, the man with the one-liner who could always quip his way out of any problem, but all she saw was anger, hatred and confusion.

"I know... *I know!*"

He brushed her off and walked out Balta's door, smashing it shut behind him. The flimsy wooden door wobbled on its hinges with the force of the blow before coming to a stop in the frame.

Hawke went to follow him but Lea caught his arm.

"Leave him," she said. "I know Ryan better than anyone. He'll be alright, but he needs time."

Hawke watched the young man through the doorway as he pounded to the end of the corridor and slumped up against the wall. "You're right – he'll come around. He's strong."

"You can say that again," Scarlet said. "Did you see the way he trounced that goon? I've never seen him fight like that before. Normally he's like a big girl's blouse but that was approaching half-decent brawling."

Lea frowned at her. "You have a real way with words, you know that, Cairo?"

Scarlet shrugged and lit a cigarette. "I was merely making an observation, darling. No need to be a cow about it."

"I'm not being a cow, I just think you should show some respect for the guy and not take the piss all the time."

"Sorry – I'm Scarlet Sloane – have we met?"

Lea rolled her eyes. "Sadly, yes."

"We haven't got time for this," Lea said. "Where are Lexi and the others?"

"They went into the other office," Hawke said.

They opened the door to see Lexi and Luis both unconscious on the floor and so sign of Balta. "There!" Lea said, leaning out the window. "They're taking him into the freaking Lollapalooza crowd!"

CHAPTER FOURTEEN

They brought Lexi and Luis around and then they all sprinted into the crowd, thousands deep, pushing their way slowly toward Kruger and his gang. Rajavi was holding a knife to Balta's throat and dragging him along the street to the south. The crowd of people walking to the festival was huge, and soon they were well away from the ECHO team.

They followed them along the Avenida Brasil and then left into the district of Orrantia del Mar, keen not to provoke Kruger into harming Balta out of panic. As Saqqal and Kruger drew further away to the south along the Circuito de Playas, Hawke knew time was running out.

They speeded up the chase and tried to stay out of sight as they pursued the enemy, but now they were moving further into the actual festival and approaching the main stage. Hawke knew as soon as they had the information about the Mandala from Balta, the professor would be a dead man.

"Where are they?" Lexi called out.

"I'm losing them!" said Scarlet.

Hawke scanned the crowd. "I think they're breaking up."

Lea flicked her head around to check the crowd only to see Saqqal a few yards to Kruger's left and getting away fast. He had less difficulty smashing partygoers out of his way than she did.

Foo Fighters were now on the stage, blasting their songs out across the heads of the festival goers who were jumping up and down to the beat and screaming along to the lyrics. Ahead of Lea the colossal speakers were blaring out a bass line she didn't recognize and one of the guitarists had his foot up on the stage-left monitor while he moshed his head up and down. The crowd were going nuts and were now jumping up and down like they were on pogo sticks.

In the chaos, she quickly became separated from Hawke and the others, and then she lost sight of the enemy. "I can't see them, Joe!" she called out.

"Leave it with me," he said.

Hawke craned his neck around for a look and then it came to him. He turned and began to climb over the security fence that divided the crowd from the stage but a second later two large men with shaved heads approached him, palms out. They were wearing bomber jackets and earpieces and he instantly clocked they were security.

They spoke to him rapidly in Spanish, and he replied in their language, but they weren't having any of it. They were the classic unmovable object, but unfortunately for them Joe Hawke was the irresistible force. He pulled back his arms and simultaneously sucker punched each of the men in the center of his face, sending them both staggering back toward the stage with broken, bloody noses.

He didn't hang about for a second round, and seized the moment he had won by leaping over the fence and using a parkour jump to launch onto the stage, landing downstage center. The bass player took a few steps back and stared at him but the band carried on as more security rushed the stage to drag him off.

He stared out over the crowd with only seconds to spare. He saw Lea and his friends straight ahead and then he saw Kruger's hat and behind him Saqqal and the professor flanked by the rebels. They were up near the stage and almost free of the crowd.

"They're over there!" he called out, but she couldn't hear him. He grabbed hold of one of the backing vocals mics and told her once again. She heard him, but so did ten thousand other people, including Kruger, and he responded by firing a warning shot into the air.

The atmosphere turned on a dime. People reacted fast, ducking their heads and screaming as they tried to move away from where they thought they'd heard the gunshot. The band stopped playing and suddenly there was security crawling everywhere like ants.

Hawke thought hanging around for the security was a bad idea so he ran along the stage and launched himself into the air. He stage-dived into the heaving throng of people and found himself crowd-surfing for a few moments until he finally clambered away from their grip and joined up with Lea.

"They're trying to head backstage," he said.

When they turned the corner and moved into the backstage area it was just in time to see Saqqal dragging a roadie out of a Wrangler while Rajavi darted around to the passenger's door. A luxury travel trailer was attached to the back of the Wrangler by the tow hook and it juddered when Saqqal fired up the Jeep and took off through the backstage area.

"I'm on it!" Lea said.

"And me," Ryan said. "I want that bastard."

Hawke watched Lea and Ryan sprinting after the stolen Wrangler while he scanned the area for the others. "Where's Kruger?" he said.

"Be fucked if I know," said Scarlet.

"Over there!" Reaper said.

He pointed to the cliffs where Kruger and Corzo were jogging along one of the coast paths. "Looks like they're heading toward the pier and they've still got Balta!"

"But no sign of Jawad," Reaper said. "This worries me."

*

While the Jeep was still in the backstage area its speed was heavily restricted by all the other trailers and tents and Lea had time to grab hold of the door on the side of the luxury travel trailer and clamber inside. She held out her hand and helped Ryan and by the time the Wrangler was leaving the area and hitting the road they were both inside.

"So what now?" Ryan asked.

"How the hell should I know?" Lea said. "This was a do now, think later scenario."

"Well, later is now," Ryan said, looking out the window. "He's picking up speed."

"Do you think he saw us get in the trailer?"

At that point the trailer began swinging wildly from one side of the road to the other and they looked through the front window to see Rajavi leaning out the Wrangler's rear window.

The trailer skidded across the lane and smashed into a supporting wall on the other side of the road, crunching the side of the trailer. Lea tried the door. "Damn thing's jammed shut now!"

Ryan watched Rajavi on the back of the Wrangler. "What the hell is he doing?"

Lea frowned as Rajavi began unscrewing the cap of the auxiliary gas tank. "I'm not liking this latest development."

They were now racing down a cliff road with the South Pacific Ocean on their left-hand side. "We must be doing at least sixty miles per hour now," Ryan said with a sigh. "Which means we're going wherever they're going."

"Er, Ry…"

"What?"

"I don't think they have that in mind."

Ryan turned to see Rajavi heaving the gas tank out of its holder and pouring the contents into a Coke bottle. Then he ripped part of his shirt off and stuffed it inside the bottle before lighting the end of the cloth and throwing it at the trailer.

Lea screamed. "Shit! A Molotov cocktail!"

They ran to the back of the trailer as the bottle smashed on the front window and burst into flames.

Trapped inside the blazing luxury travel trailer, Lea searched for something to put through the window, but all the heavy stuff like chairs and tables were fixed into place so she went to the kitchen area and opened one of the drawers, snatching out a frying pan. The sound of the Foo Fighters was still loud in the air and the crowd was singing along as loud as they could as she shielded her eyes and swung the pan at the small window.

It bounced back hard and heavy, the failed attempt reverberating harshly up her arm. The window was thick Perspex and no travel-size frying pan was going to break it.

The trailer bounced around violently now, and Lea cupped her hands on the window to see what was going on. They were skidding dangerously close to the edge of the cliff and the flames were spreading all over the trailer.

"Bugger it sideways!" she said, flinging the pan across the trailer and putting her hands on her hips. She had to think about this.

The fire grew in strength, and they watched in horror as the flames licked up the sides and over the windows. "It's going to start getting hot in here," she said.

"You think?" Ryan said.

"What the hell are we going to do?"

"Get out of here, that's what."

CHAPTER FIFTEEN

Hawke, Reaper, Lexi, Scarlet and Luis jogged down the track in pursuit of Kruger, Corzo, Balta and the rebels. They were now running along the Miraflores Pier and heading toward the Rosa Nautica restaurant. Hawke could see dozens of passers-by moving quickly away from the men as they dragged the old professor down the pier at knifepoint, but there were no police in sight. Only they could save Balta now.

"Come on!" Hawke yelled. "We've almost got them."

They crossed the Circuito de Playas and hit the pier, sprinting as fast as they could toward the Rosa Nautica. "There they are!"

Inside the restaurant was a picture of serene calm as diners chinked glasses of wine and enjoyed their meals, but then Joe Hawke arrived and things changed rapidly.

Kruger and Corzo were making their way toward the kitchen door when they saw the ECHO team, and their response was to pull their guns and fire into the ceiling. The customers created instantly in a burst of screams and panic. Some dived under tables while others bolted for the door.

Hawke ran toward the kitchen but Carlos Corzo appeared from behind a support pillar and surprised him with a straight-forward shovel hook.

Hawke stumbled back into a table directly behind and tipped it up, spraying lobster and salad all over the place. The shell from the cracked claws rained down on the head of a woman who was hiding behind a tropical fish tank and she screamed inconsolably as it stuck to her hair and fell down her neck.

"I'm terribly sorry," Hawke said. "I'm sure the management could probably refund your dinner, at a pinch."

Scarlet shook her head and rolled her eyes. "Pay for it yourself and stop being shellfish."

"Very good," Hawke said, but the rest of his reply was cut short when Corzo grabbed him around the collar and yanked him away from the detritus of the collapsed table. The Englishman staggered to his feet and planted a hefty smack on his jaw. He went back and gouged his back against the corner of a table.

Across the restaurant, Dirk Kruger was walking backward toward the kitchen door while letting rip with an Uzi in his other hand. He sprayed bullets wildly but they all missed their mark. *Amateur*, Hawke thought. The bullets hit a fire extinguisher and suddenly the room was filled with a thick cloud of CO_2. Customers piled all over the place like startled antelopes, but Hawke's eyes were on the job.

Kruger raked another line of fire over the busy room, and screamed at Hawke to back off. Reaper leaped forward and punched Kruger from the side, knocking him back through another of the tropical fish tanks and sending him sliding about in the water on the floor. The South African was dazed for a few moments before getting back to his feet and snatching his bag up.

He grabbed his gun and raked the chaotic restaurant with more bullets before darting away into the cloud of CO_2. The ECHO team dived to the floor and Hawke's mind raced to keep control of the situation. Between the CO_2, the gunfire and the dust from the blasted ceiling tiles, the restaurant had become a House of Horrors. He heard Kruger yelling in Afrikaans from the kitchens – presumably trying to locate Corzo.

The Colombian scrambled to his feet and grabbed Balta. Snatching a knife off one of the tables, he held it to the professor's throat. "Step back or he dies. Dies!" He pushed the knife into the terrified man's throat. It was only a butter knife, but Hawke knew it would easily go through the skin with the sort of effort Corzo was prepared to supply and then Balta was a dead man.

Hawke took a step back and raised his hands to show he was backing off, and Corzo started to drag Balta back toward the kitchen door where they joined Kruger and disappeared.

Hawke and the others sprinted across the restaurant and into the kitchens where they found themselves looking at several terrified chefs who were hiding behind the industrial ovens. One of them looked at Hawke and raised a trembling hand to point at a swinging door on the far side of the large room.

They ran to it and sprinted down a corridor. At the end was the fire exit Kruger and Corzo had used to take Balta and flee the restaurant. They scrambled through it and found themselves outside on the pier.

The merciless Peruvian sun pitched down on him and he raised his hand to shield his eyes but when they had adjusted he realized too late what Kruger's plan had been.

Jawad was racing across the water on a motorboat from further up the coast. He pulled up alongside the pier and after forcing Balta into the boat, Kruger and Corzo jumped down into it behind him.

Kruger gave Hawke a cheery wave as Jawad turned the boat to starboard and opened the throttles. Moments later they were a kilometre up the coast.

Hawke felt the rage rise. He padded up the pier and tried to slow his breathing. "Damn it! They got Balta!"

Reaper cleared his throat. "Yes, but we got the mask."

"Eh?"

"I got it when I punched Kruger through the fish tank. He was too shaken up to check his little bag when he took off."

"That's great, Reap," Hawke said, but still angry. "But if he has Balta then he doesn't need the mask."

*

Ryan yanked at the table. It was bolted down but when he started booting it the bolts started to loosen. "By the way," he said, planting another kick on the table. "I've decided to pack all this shit in."

"What shit?"

"The aforementioned ECHO shit. I've had enough."

"You can't do that, Ry. What else have you got? Think it through."

He smashed the table with his boot and this time it came away. "Just watch me."

He lifted the table over to the door and began using it as a battering ram to smash at the door. The first ramming didn't leave a mark.

"At first I was sceptical, especially about Joe, but then I started to enjoy it."

"So? What's the problem then?"

"The problem is that after I lost Sophie I nearly quit, and now Maria is gone there's nothing for me here anymore. I want time alone and then a new life. Not this anymore... All the jetting about and getting shot at. I don't want it."

He rammed the door a second time and buckled it out in the frame. "Thank god for that," he said, wiping some sweat from his eyes. "This place is like an oven and when the flames reach the cooking gas we'll be the first people on the moon since 1972."

Another smash and the sound of metal bending. Something inside the lock pinged and the door began to give way.

"At least talk to everyone else about it when we get back to Elysium."

He looked at her. "And what's waiting for me there, except Maria's grave?"

She had no words.

The door popped open and flames instantly licked their way all around the frame and began to climb inside the trailer. "Shield yourself!" he said, taking hold of her arm. "We're outta here."

"Wait a minute," Lea said, horrified.

Ryan looked at her. "What is it?"

"Rajavi's disconnecting the sodding trailer!"

Outside Rajavi had now opened the rear tailgate completely and was disconnecting the trailer from the Wrangler.

"We're going over that cliff in about ten seconds,' Lea said. "It's now or never!"

They leaped out the trailer just as it careered over the cliff and a heartbeat later it exploded in a savage fireball, blasting an enormous cloud of detritus and debris all over the road and cliff.

"Janey Bloody Mac!" Lea yelled as she tumbled over and came to a halt on the grass at the edge of the cliff.

Ryan came to a halt a few yards away and took a breath. "Turns out we're not going to the moon just yet."

CHAPTER SIXTEEN

The area known in Mandarin as Dong Jiaomin Xiang, but to the West as the Beijing Legation Quarter was in the very heart of the enormous, sprawling Chinese capital. It contained many of China's most famous landmarks and buildings, including the Great Hall of the People, the Mausoleum of Mao Zedong and Tiananmen Square.

It also contained the headquarters of the Chinese Ministry of State Security.

The vast building was close to the Forbidden City, but the tourists rarely went south of the Tongzi River, and the building's purpose was unknown even to most Beijingers. The machinations whirring behind its heavy doors were some of the most secretive on earth, and if the Guojia Anquan Bu, or Guoanbu, didn't want you to know what they were doing, you didn't know.

In an unassuming corner office somewhere in the building's northeast, a thin man in a boring suit buzzed for his personal assistant and moments later she showed another man into the room. The second man had slicked-back hair and a small scar contracture below his lower lip. He nodded his head respectfully at the man in the boring suit and after being invited to take a seat he lowered himself into the uncomfortable wooden chair opposite the desk.

"Good morning, sir," said the man with the scar.

"You are over two minutes late."

"I apologize."

The man in the boring suit, whose name was Zhou Yang, was the second in command of the General Office of the Central Investigation Department. He also ran a small subdivision of ruthless assassins informally named the Zodiac Syndicate. Sitting opposite him, with the scar, was the man they called Tiger. Zhou had long forgotten his real name and would have to search his files to retrieve it, something he was not particularly inclined to do this morning.

"Have you found her?" Zhou said quietly.

"Yes, sir. She is working with an independent Western agency."

"Based where – London?"

Tiger shook his head. "Not London, but we don't know beyond that."

"Last known location?"

"Cartagena."

Zhou nodded, unsurprised. "The little dragonfly has flown to Colombia, I see."

"Your orders?"

"She is to be terminated, and so are any of her associates. We do not know what she has told them and we do not take risks."

"Yes, sir."

"Make sure you take only your best people with you."

"Of course, sir."

"I await your final report with restrained excitement."

Tiger rose from is chair, bowed to the man and left the office. By the time he had closed the door Zhou was already on his feet and peering out his little window across the enormous courtyard at the center of the Ministry's sprawling compound.

It was too bad the Dragonfly had betrayed him. Once she had been a loyal servant of the State and it was with disappointment that he had ordered her death. Such a beautiful and merciless creature as that would have had a glowing career ahead of her at the Ministry, but crossing him was unforgivable, and in their trade letting her live would be bad etiquette so he had no choice.

He sighed and buzzed his personal assistant again.

"Yes, sir?"

"One cup of white tea, please."

"Yes, sir."

He cut the connection and nodded his head slowly.

Very bad etiquette indeed.

CHAPTER SEVENTEEN

Back at their hotel in Lima, the ECHO team and Luis Montoya grabbed a few cold beers and took stock of the mission. This was the first real chance any of them had to think about Ryan Bale surviving the Seastead battle and being back in the team, but it was bittersweet because of Maria's death. They had also lost Professor Balta to Saqqal and Kruger, but they had finally got hold of the infamous Mask of Inti.

Now, they stared at the ancient golden mask in awe. It was vaguely circular and around twelve inches in diameter, formed into what was clearly a burning sun, with wild flames around the outside. In the center was a rendering of the face of Inti himself. He stared back at them with blank gold eyes and elongated, decorated ears.

Thanks to gold being the least reactive metal, no oxides had formed on the mask, so despite its ancient provenance it was still as glorious as the day it had been forged by the Incan goldsmith. Scarlet especially had a hard time keeping her eyes off it.

"You all right, Cairo?" Hawke asked.

"Why do you ask?"

"It's that the way you're looking at old Inti there I wondered if you two wanted to be alone for an hour."

"An hour? Don't judge everyone by your own standards, darling."

He gave her a wry smile but turned away to face the Peruvian. "We're going to need your help now, Luis."

"Golden masks were very common in Inca legend," Luis began. "Gold played an enormous part in their culture because they believed it was literally the sun's sweat. They would use it for all kinds of jewellery and ornaments and they would beat it down into thin sheets and make plates, disks and of course masks from it."

"No wonder the Spanish thought they'd hit the jackpot." Lexi said.

"I'll say," said Scarlet, unable to take her eyes of the glittering mask.

Luis frowned. "The pillage of Inca treasure by the Spanish is a sad story full of violence and theft. When Francisco Pizarro led his conquistadors into the Inca lands back in the early 1530s and took Atahualpa prisoner, it is true that they couldn't believe how much gold was here. Even today Peru is one of the largest gold-producing nations in the world."

Scarlet walked to the balcony and looked out over the city. She let out a long sigh as she lit a cigarette. "I've finally found home."

Luis glanced at her. "For most of the people in my country, Peru has a very low standard of living by most Western standards."

Hawke cleared his throat. "Let's get back to the mask."

"As I was saying, it was previously thought that Pizarro held Atahualpa hostage until a ransom was paid, and because he was such a mighty emperor, they got their blackmail money. His people delivered more gold and silver than the Spanish had ever seen before – historians claim it was more than could be carried by fifteen thousand Incas – and the invaders happily took it all, including presumably this mask. Today we think it more likely that Atahualpa offered the incredible amount of treasure simply as a way to keep himself alive."

100

"Did it work?" Reaper asked.

Luis shook his head. "It definitely did *not* work. Atahualpa's generals, including the famous Rumiñawi continued to make war against the Spanish in a bid to free their emperor, so Pizarro staged a show trial for Atahualpa and found him guilty of rebellion. He was sentenced to be burned to death."

"Bloody hell," Scarlet said.

"An especially wicked sentence because it was the Inca's belief that if you were burned to death your soul would not reach the afterlife. Luckily for Atahualpa, a Spanish friar managed to persuade Pizarro to reduce the sentence and he was garrotted to death."

Lexi raised an eyebrow. "Yes, that does sound lucky."

"I know what you mean," Luis said with a smile. "But it was lucky for the emperor because at least that way his soul could go to the Hanan Pacha, their concept of heaven."

"Anything else we need to know?" Hawke said.

Luis shrugged his shoulders. "Many years after Atahualpa's death, another Spaniard named Valverde got married to a princess of the same Inca tribe and according to legend she took him to the famous lost treasure – the greatest collection of plates, goblets, salvers and sculptures ever created. The legend said he became very wealthy overnight and then returned to Spain where he wrote what is now known as the Derrotero de Valverde, or Valverde's Path in which he carefully described how to find the treasure."

"But obviously no luck?" Lea asked.

"None at all. After Valverde died he bequeathed the map to King Charles V of Spain who in turn sent the map back to South America and ordered a renewed search for the rest of the treasure. Sadly, all expeditions to find the treasure using Valverde's Path led to nothing but strange disappearances and deaths… unless you count the Blake and Chapman expedition."

"Do tell," Scarlet said.

"In 1857, a British botanist named Richard Spruce was on a scientific expedition to discover new plants. He was in South America with the hope of finding a malaria cure when he stumbled upon the map sent there hundreds of years earlier by King Charles. Through a series of conversations over many years, the map ended up in the hands of two Royal Navy sailors named Captain Blake and Lieutenant Chapman."

"This is getting sexier by the second," Scarlet said.

"Don't get too excited," Luis said. "Soon into the treasure hunting expedition Captain Blake died and they buried him in the Andes but Chapman returned to his ship claiming he had found the treasure and he brought samples to prove it. He left the map with a friend called Albertson in Boston while he took the samples to London for appraisal by the British Museum and then planned to return with a team to find the treasure, except he fell overboard on his way to Albertson in Boston and died."

"I see what you mean about everyone who searches for this treasure dying," Lea said.

"So where's the map?" Hawke asked.

"No one knows. Albertson in Boston was the last person to hold it – if indeed it ever existed. I think with the discovery of this mask we have a much better chance of finding the treasure than anyone with Valverde's Path."

Lexi picked up the mask and held it in front of her face for a moment, looking through the eyeholes at the others. "I am your god!" she said.

Luis took it away from her with a frown. "This mask is clearly a priceless work of art simply for its historical and archaeological significance," he said, "but the merest suggestion that it might contain some kind of clue to the location of Paititi raises its importance to the highest level. This mask could potentially be the greatest archaeological discovery in the history of our country, and maybe the world if the rumors about Paititi are even halfway true. I must say, I still have my doubts, although I am being persuaded slowly that perhaps the Lost City exists after all."

"We're not there yet," Hawke said, taking the mask and turning it over in his hands.

"No, but this is still an amazing artefact. Until the raising of the galleon no one had ever seen it before so this is the first time anyone has really had a chance to see if they are more than mere legends."

"The second time," Hawke said with regret. "Kruger's already had his filthy mitts on it so we have to work fast."

"Of course," said the young Peruvian.

"So where are we going next?" Scarlet said.

"Remember what Balta said," Lea said. "About the mask's reference to the Nazca Lines?" She called up Google Earth and they zoomed in on the Nazca Lines. Moments later they found the Mandala glyph.

"Professor Balta told us that these pictograms told us we have to *Follow the Sun, Cross and Sacred Stone and The Tomb of Pachacuti will illuminate the Path to Paititi.*'"

"He also told us no one knows where the Tomb of Pachacuti is," Lexi said.

"No, that's not right," Lea said. "He told us the location of the tomb is disputed."

"That's correct," Luis said. "Some say Machu Picchu but others say Toqocachi, near San Blas."

"So how does this Mandala thing in the Nazca Lines help us?" Hawke said.

"Balta said it could be some kind of compass."

They stared at the Mandala again. Do you remember that Balta said he thought we had to line up the sun and the cross of this thing and it would point us in the right direction?"

Hawke nodded. "Use the tool to draw a line through the cross and sun."

Lea selected the line tool and made the line. "All right – it's going straight though the middle of the cross and sun, which is making a bearing of about sixty degrees or so. Now what?"

"Balta said it was Fifty Tupus," Luis said.

Scarlet giggled. "And I think Fifty Tupus…"

Hawke raised his hand. "Don't even *think* it, Cairo."

"Where does it lead?" Reaper said, leaning over Lea's shoulder.

"Funnily enough," the young Irishwoman began, "the dropdown menu on Google Earth doesn't feature any ancient Incan terms of measurement."

From beside Scarlet on the balcony Ryan called over his shoulder. "It's about three hundred and thirty kilometres."

Scarlet twisted her head and faced him. "Christ almighty, Ryan – you really are full of useless drivel."

"Thanks."

Lea selected kilometres and a second later her eyes widened like two saucers. "I guess that's pretty unambiguous then."

Hawke stared down at the iPhone screen. "Machu Picchu… Pachacuti's tomb is at Machu Picchu after all."

"But look carefully," Luis said. "The line is going just north of the ancient citadel. I don't think this is a calculation error. I think the entrance to the tomb is just outside the city."

Scarlet blew out the last of her cigarette smoke and flicked the butt off the balcony. Ryan also turned and they each came back inside the room. "Let's stop pissing about then and get there," she said. "Kruger will have beaten this out of Balta by now and he's probably already halfway there."

CHAPTER EIGHTEEN

On the flight from Lima to Cusco, Hawke felt jumpy and tired. There was still no word about Eden's condition back in London and every time he closed his eyes he saw Maria, the young Russian woman savagely cut down in her prime.

He tried to bring himself back on message by swearing for the hundredth time that he would bury Kruger's bones if it was the last thing he ever did, but every time reality crawled up from the pit of his despair and clawed at his conscience until he felt bad all over again. At least Ryan was here, alive and well. But he had changed, and this time Hawke knew it was forever.

He looked over at Lea but turned away and shut his eyes before she noticed. He couldn't tell what she was thinking anymore, and it felt like she was drifting away. Or maybe he was the one drifting. He didn't know. It was obvious everyone was feeling the pressure of the losses of the Atlantis mission. Reaper was sleeping on the couch in the center of the small jet and Luis was reading through the professor's files opposite him, but Lexi and Scarlet were sitting at the table in the rear of the jet and arguing. They'd been grumbling for a while, but now their voices were rising in volume.

"Hey!" Lea shouted, keeping her head facing forward. "Trying to get some sleep up here!"

"Come down here then and I'll slap you to sleep," Scarlet said.

"Hey – what are you chewing?" Ryan asked Scarlet.

"Acullico. Want some, *boy?*"

He nodded and she passed him some. He put it in his mouth and started to chew. "What the hell is this stuff?"

"Coca," she said flatly. "Grabbed me some back in Lima."

"Bloody hell!" Ryan said. "You could have told me."

"You should know not to accept strange things from strange people by now, Ry," Lea said.

"Spit it out if you don't like it," Scarlet said.

Ryan closed his eyes and carried on chewing. "No, you're all right."

"Get some rest, everyone," Hawke said. Thankfully they listened to him and quietened down. He was losing focus and the squabbling of his team as they slowly unwound wasn't helping him get things back together one little bit. Any thoughts he'd vaguely circled about quitting ECHO were destroyed the second Eden went into the coma.

How could he walk away from his friends and leave them without a leader? But the truth was he wasn't sure he could lead them, at least not back on the island. His skills were all in the field. He had no idea of how Eden funded ECHO, or who or what the Consortium was. He looked around the cabin and realized he didn't even know how Eden paid for jet fuel.

The fact Eden took care of the strategic level while he focussed on tactics in the field was why it all worked so well, not to mention Ryan's brilliant polymath mind that was so adept at finding patterns in the chaos. The truth was the team had been smashed but he still had to pick up the pieces and try and move forward.

He used the new peace to focus on the mission again. The Lost Inca Gold was probably the greatest missing hoard in the world. No other treasure was so infamous and so cloaked in mystery and the lust for wealth and power. People had been searching for it for hundreds and hundreds of years, and dozens of expeditions had been commissioned into the jungles of Peru, Bolivia and Brazil just in the last century. While these things excited him, they also highlighted just how unrealistic it was that they were going to have any more luck than all the previous failures.

At least they had decoded the cryptic inscription and symbols on the Mask of Inti. This alone meant they had a better chance than most of the treasure hunters who had gone before. He thought about Professor Balta now in Kruger's hands, and what they might have done to him to make him spill the beans on the location. He prayed Balta was still alive and decided to try and get some sleep before they touched down at Cusco Airport. From there he would be piloting a hired chopper into the foothills of the Andes.

*

Lexi Zhang was dreaming. She was sitting in the back room of her parents' home and watching her mother grind ink. She had just finished washing the tea inkstick and was now ready to grind the inkstone. First she poured some water into the grindstone and then unwrapped the block of tea ink and began to grind it into the water.

How many times she had watched this didn't matter, because in this dream it was happening now, and she was just a child. She watched as the black tea-stained pigment pushed out into the water, slowly getting thicker as her mother pushed the stick around the small green Duan inkstone.

The sunlight illuminated dust motes as they danced around her mother's face but she was concentrating too much on the ink's consistency to notice any distraction.

Outside in the yard she heard the gentle call of a hawfinch as it hopped around their neighbor's pear tree. She loved that tree. It reminded her of morning walks around Xiangshui Lake.

When the ink was ready, her mother selected a soft calligraphy brush and began to write the poem on the paper.

It was so peaceful, she thought.

What happened to my life?

Her mother began to fade, and she was suddenly aware of her surroundings on board the Gulfstream. The gentle grinding of the inkstone and the hawfinch's song now replaced by the hum of the air-conditioning and the white noise roar of the air outside as the plane cut through it at a thousand kilometres per hour. She wanted to go back to sleep, but she yawned and stretched her arms over her head instead. Real life never went away just because you wanted it to, and somewhere down there Dirk Kruger had to be stopped.

CHAPTER NINETEEN

Machu Picchu

Hawke flew the team from Alejandro Velasco Astete Airport in Cusco through the meandering valleys of the Urubamba River. At the end of the flight he increased altitude to fly over the top of a high peak to the south of the small town of Aguas Calientes and then they were all shocked to see the incredible site of Machu Picchu, perched on the backbone of a mountain ridge in the middle of the mountains.

It was unlike anything any of them had ever seen before – a magnificent citadel of ancient ruins in the total isolation of the Urubamba Mountains. Clouds drifted in the valleys below and the whole site was bewitchingly timeless as they drew closer to its crumbling walls and plazas.

He flew on, overpassing the Gate of the Sun and then descended over the southern slopes which lead to the ancient city. Its honey-colored ruins shone in the bright Peruvian sun, highlighted in stark contrast to the luscious emerald greens of the mountainous jungle enveloping it on all sides.

He flew over the top of the ancient guardhouse, the main gate, the sacred plaza and finally intiwatana, the old astronomic clock, before flaring the chopper's nose and bringing the machine down to the north of the ancient Inca citadel, a few yards away from the Sacred Rock.

After hovering the chopper above the ruins – and more than a few bemused tourists – Hawke found his landing place, and lowered the collective, reducing power to the rotor engine. He brought the helicopter to a gentle touchdown in a plaza at the northern end of what five hundred years ago had been the urban sector and moments later they were jumping out and emerging into an ancient world.

They cleared the slowing rotors and gathered once again to read the compass before heading off due north, just as the markings on the Mask of Inti had told them to. As they had expected from another study of Google Earth on the way, the mask was leading them out of the citadel itself and into the jungle to the north of it.

A thin white mist floated up from the valley and began to shroud some of the lower reaches of the citadel and then formed into full clouds.

"We're above the clouds," Lexi said.

Far across on the mountain to the south they watched yet another group of tourists as they ambled around the Gate of the Sun with their cameras before heading back down to Cusco with their memories and their photos.

Lea tried to take it all in but it was like nothing she had ever seen before in her entire life. The air was indescribably fresh, and the sensation of the clouds moving through the valley below her almost made her feel as if it were the mountains moving and the clouds were nothing more than a static sea.

She linked her arm through Hawke's. "Can't we give up all of this and just stay here forever?"

"I would, but you do realize there's no TV up here?"

"What?"

Hawke nodded. "Sad but true."

"Maybe it's not such a great idea in that case."

She glanced over her shoulder at the tourists who were now walking up through the ruins to get a closer look at the helicopter. Following up behind them were a couple of workers from the tourist center. "We're drawing some attention, guys."

"When do we *not* draw attention?" Scarlet said, casually pulling a cigarette from her pocket and firing it up.

Hawke glanced back and took in the tourists once again, amazed by the number of people who had made the laborious trek via trains and hiking to get up here. They swarmed all over the mountain, but for the most part maintained a respectful silence as they took it all in.

He turned and surveyed the ruined citadel from up close and was instantly struck by how much larger it was in reality compared with the many pictures and films he had seen of it over the course of his life. It seemed to tumble and stretch all over the mountain in whatever direction he looked. Here, enormous stone steps leading up to a ruined temple, there, a smooth plaza covered in páramo grass, and at every turn another huddle of tourists in sun hats taking selfies of themselves in front of the incredible citadel.

He also noticed the almost precipitous drop off the west side of the ruins. One false step over there and it was Goodnight Vienna but not before a long and desperate rough and tumble all the way down to the Urubamba River hundreds of feet below.

"Maybe we should be a bit more subtle about this?" Luis said, looking at the tourists and guides.

Ryan scoffed. "Screw them."

Hawke looked at him but turned away. The last thing Ryan needed now was someone getting too close. "We keep going," he said, as Luis joined him at the front. "We must be nearly there by now."

"So we've done the Fifty Tupus," Luis said, causing Scarlet to laugh and shake her head in amusement. "Now for the Fifty Rikras."

They headed to the Sacred Stone and Luis began to count out the distance as Lexi measured their progress on GPS. They left the citadel and started walking into the jungle.

The sunlight pierced the canopy of the mahogany and yarumo trees as they pushed through the subtropical vegetation all around them. Though a gap in the trees they saw a strip of páramo grass and then the low growling of a tiger heron drifted out from some hidden quarter. A hummingbird flashed past on its way to a vine.

"So you're sure of how long a *rikra* was?" Hawke asked Luis.

The Peruvian nodded. "There's no doubt. One *rikra* was just over a meter and a half. There are very clear descriptions of it in Incan architecture."

"And which way are we going?" Lea asked,

"The line from the Mandala ran to the north, so the answer is we're almost right on top of it."

They walked on through the jungle and looked around for clues. The walk from Machu Picchu had been down hill, so now they could no longer see the ruined citadel jutting through the jungle canopy.

Dense jungle surrounded them on all sides. Hawke waved a sandfly from his face and surveyed the landscape. "Looks like mostly coca and even some coffee."

"Please, don't talk to me about coffee trees," Lea said. "I had enough of those in Mexico to last me fifty lifetimes."

"Talking of fifty," Lexi said. "We're now exactly fifty *rikras* due north of the Sacred Rock."

They stopped and began to search for anything that might be a lead, but the only obvious answer was a broken slab of granite.

Lea kicked it with her boot. "This boy looks a little out of place, wouldn't ya say?"

"It's probably just a piece of stone rejected for the main construction," Luis said, crouching to get a better look at it. "The city was made from granite and also some limestone, constructed with ashlar masonry, a technique to create square blocks which are then smoothed with sand. It was very precise work as you can see from the ruins and it looks like an error was made on this piece so they threw it out."

"You guys are thinking what I'm thinking, right?" Lea said with a grin.

Hawke nodded and returned the smile. "Oh yeah."

"What?" Luis asked innocently.

Reaper clapped his arm around Luis's shoulder. "It's not that we doubt your theory of the stone being rejected," he said, roll-up bouncing on his lower lip as he spoke. "But we think maybe this is here for another reason."

The young Peruvian archaeologist looked confused. "I don't understand."

"They used it to conceal the entrance to the tomb, *Looo*-is," Scarlet said, still chewing the acullico. She was stepping from foot to foot, pumped by the coca and excited by what was going to happen next. "I take it we have the goods?"

Hawke nodded. "The usual – some C4 and a few blasting caps."

"Wait," Luis said, the horror slowly rising in his voice. "C4 is an explosive isn't it?"

"It sure is," Scarlet said.

"We like blowing things up," Ryan said. "Get used to it."

"You can't seriously be proposing to blow up this piece of granite just to see what's underneath? This is part of one of the most important World Heritage Sites!"

Scarlet rolled her eyes. "Been there, done it, and stained the t-shirt."

"We could destroy valuable archaeological evidence, not to mention the obvious criminal prosecution such an act would demand."

"Maybe he's right," Lexi said.

Luis turned to her, hope returning to his eyes. "Really?"

"Of course not," the Chinese assassin said. "If you're frightened of loud noises I'd go over there behind those trees for a few minutes and put your fingers in your ears."

"I am *not* frightened of loud noises so I'll be staying right here with all of you."

"With us?" Hawke said as he pulled the C4 out his bag and fixed it in the crack where the granite dug into the earth. "We're going over there behind those trees with our fingers in our ears."

"Ah."

"All right, let's go."

They moved twenty meters to the west and crouched behind a low ridge for cover. When everyone was safe and Hawke knew the blast zone was clear, he detonated the explosives.

The sound of the explosion roared out in the heavy silence of the Historic Sanctuary of Machu Picchu and echoed off dozens of neighboring mountainsides. Flocks of nightjars, hummingbirds and cinnamon flycatchers took to the air in terror as the violent noise rang out through the valleys below, but only when the shredded canopy of pisonay and alder fell to earth in a shower of splintered granite over their heads did they hear the sound of human screams in response to the detonation. The tourists back up in Machu Picchu were obviously panicking about what had happened, but they had all expected that response.

"Looks like the countdown has begun," Lea said.

"So let's get going," Hawke said.

"What about death traps?" Lexi said.

Luis shook his head. "Incas were actually quite a peaceful people, which is why many speculate they were destroyed and vanished so quickly. They weren't anywhere near as dangerous and bloodthirsty as the Aztecs."

"That's a relief," Lea said. "I've had enough of Aztecs, thanks very much."

They clambered to their feet and jogged back down the slope to where the granite block had been, but now they were looking at a smoking hole in the jungle floor.

"That's our boy!" Lea said. "I presume you're going first, Luis?"

"What?"

"You being the only fully trained archaeologist and all."

"Well, I…"

"She's pulling your leg," Hawke said, pulling a Maglite from his canvas bag and switching it on. He shook his head with amusement as he lowered himself down in the black hole.

CHAPTER TWENTY

The tunnel was extremely narrow and in places their shoulders scraped against the carved walls as they moved through it. They quickly worked out they were walking uphill, and it became obvious where it was leading thanks to the due-south direction compass reading – back to Machu Picchu.

"It's leading us right back to the citadel," Hawke said, shining his flashlight into the pitch-black gloom. Walking up the hill was hard work because the tunnel seemed steeper than the path above them, but at least the tunnel was widening now.

"Thank heaven for small mercies," Lea said, finally able to move up and walk alongside Hawke. "It was less than a hundred yards so we should be there in no time, and then – hang on."

"What is it?" Lexi called out from behind.

Ryan gave a bitter laugh. "It's a dead-end. Like my life."

"Easy, mate," Hawke said.

"You're absolutely totally completely fucking kidding?" Scarlet said with a sigh.

"Take a look."

Hawke shone the light ahead and they all saw the same thing – a solid stone wall blocking the path.

"That's just arsing fantastic," Lea said, pulling her hair back with a sigh.

Hawke wiped the sweat from his face and approached the wall. "Luis – get up here!"

The Peruvian moved cautiously forward until he was standing beside Hawke. "What is it?"

"Looks like some kind of markings. Please tell me they mean something that can get us through this wall."

Luis Montoya immediately saw what the Englishman was talking about. Carved into the walls were several simple bas-relief pictographs similar to the ones on the Mask of Inti. Thanks to their protected environment they were as crisp as they day they had been made and Luis was in awe as he passed his hands over them. "These are exquisite."

"Can you translate them?"

"I think so, but I'm no Balta. This first one is easy – it looks to me like a depiction of Supay, the Incan god of death and the lord of Ukhu Pacha."

The ECHO team shared an anxious glance behind Luis's back. "Go on," Hawke said.

"Even today the Quechua people observe traditional dances designed to appease him but this depiction is slightly unusual because it seems to indicate that…wait – according to Incan mythology, Unu Pachakuti was a terrible flood caused by Viracocha, the father god. It killed all the tribes living around Lake Titicaca leaving only two people alive so the world could repopulate."

"I've a seen similar story elsewhere…" Lea said.

"The point is I think these carvings are not only a warning but some kind of test. If we get it wrong the tunnel will flood."

Scarlet stared at him. "I thought you said the Incas were a peaceful people, Teach?"

Luis returned a nervous glance. "Well…"

"Flood?" Lexi asked. "How's that possible? I don't see any water around here."

"Machu Picchu had access to plentiful underground water supplies. Back when it was a thriving city the inhabitants enjoyed flowing water which they collected from fountains. My guess is that this door is connected to the very same water supply that the inhabitants of the citadel used every day for their survival, and that if we fail the test it will unleash some kind of flood. Maybe not on the same scale as Uni Pachakuti, but how big would it really have to be to kill some people in an underground tunnel of this size?"

They shared another worried glance.

"So if you get the combination wrong the tunnel ceiling collapses and we get flooded all the way to hell?" Scarlet said. "Sounds fair and reasonable. Anyone got any more coca?"

"No," Hawke said with a sideways glance. "And I think that's just as well, don't you, Cairo?"

Luis carefully pushed each bas-relief carving in turn and they waited nervously to see if he had gotten it right. With the last one now pushed back into the wall, they heard a deep, grinding sound and then finally the stone wall in front of them lowered into a slit in the ground.

"It's using gravity to open," Luis said. "Absolute genius!"

"Boring," said Ryan.

"So where's the water?" Lexi said, still sceptical.

Hawke shone his Maglite into the newly opened section of corridor and then up onto its ceiling.

"It's not carved rock any more," he said, staring up at the new tunnel. "But the same smooth granite blocks that we saw back in the citadel."

"That's because we're now under the citadel," Luis said. "Wait – shine the flashlight over there. Is that water?"

Hawke moved the light and saw the archaeologist was right. The new section of tunnel that the test had revealed was more of a corridor, with its floor, walls and ceiling constructed of smooth granite blocks instead of carved bedrock, but more than that the ceiling blocks were damp and here and there along the walls water was running down onto the floor.

"We must be beneath some kind of artificial aquifer," Hawke said. He turned to Luis and patted him on the shoulder. "I think you were right. If you'd cocked up that test we'd all be drowning round about now."

Hawke took another look at the water and knew they had to move fast. It must have been like this for centuries, but this was the first time anyone had walked through here. He had no idea what their presence might trigger or if there were any more booby-traps. A quick calculation told him than thanks to his SBS training he could probably hold his breath and make it out again, but he knew the others might not be so lucky, and that was presuming the trap didn't include the other end of the tunnel being blocked as well.

"Let's keep going," Hawke said cheerfully. "It's not beer o'clock yet, you bloody layabouts."

Lea laughed, and they made their forward deeper into the passage. "Here's to hopin' there ain't no more booby traps."

"Seconded," said Scarlet.

They moved further along the passage, noticing there were an increasing number of the strange pictographs as they got closer to the citadel. The granite they had used to construct the tunnel was as smooth as marble, but the limestone above it where they'd carved the symbols was rougher. "This must be the highlight of my career," Luis mumbled, excited by the ancient carvings. "Of my life!"

"Sounds like you might need a night out with Cairo," Hawke said casually.

"Half an hour would do it, surely," Lea added.

From behind them in the tunnel they heard the sound of Scarlet doing her best sarcastic laugh.

At the end of the passage was what they were looking for – a small pyramid temple with some kind of shrine at the top. Hawke moved ahead and climbed up the side of the pyramid on all fours until he reached the top. He turned and smiled at them. "Seems like the Mask's not just decorative."

"What do you mean?" Lea said. Her voice echoed in the cold chamber.

"Looks like it could be a key. Bring it up."

*

Kruger's Sikorsky S76 swept though the valley at speed before slowing for its final approach over Machu Picchu. Saqqal rubbed his nose in an attempt to look casual as the South African flared the nose and brought the machine to a sudden, jolting hover, but the truth was he hated flying and was feeling nervous. "Are we landing now?" he asked.

Kruger ignored the question, but instead spoke into his headset. "When we hit the ground I want all men out of this chopper and fanning out, no fucking about." He turned and gave Balta a sneer. "Any funny business from you, professor, and you're going into that ravine, got it?"

Balta was unable to speak because of the gag, but he nodded his head to show he got it as Kruger continued to lower the chopper. In the citadel were the usual groups of tourists milling around taking selfies and appreciating the mountain air, but what had changed Kruger's mood was the small group gathering around a Bell which was parked on some kind of plaza in the far north. "Bastards got here first."

He lowered the collective and reduced the power, bringing the chopper down through the humid air and into the ruins of the citadel's urban sector. Seconds later, the chopper's rubber tires were gently pushing into the grass. Moments later a Huey Venom filled with the CGF rebels landed beside it.

"Go, go, go!" Kruger yelled, and unbuckled himself before pulling a submachine gun from beside his seat and climbing out. The gun was shouldered before his boots had hit the earth, and he watched critically as the men fanned out and took cover behind various broken-down walls.

"All right, General," Kruger said. "You and the Professor here are to follow me."

Not used to being spoken to in this way, Saqqal bristled but said nothing. The truth was he had come to Kruger because he needed him, and for now that meant keeping his mouth shut. He jumped out the chopper and followed the South African. Rajavi, Corzo and Jawad were a few paces behind them.

Settled in behind the Temple of the Sun, Kruger pulled a pair of binoculars to his eyes and surveyed the area for a few seconds. "Don't want any nasty surprises."

"Like what?" Jawad said.

"Like the way a cat leaves a shit behind the sofa, Professor."

"I don't understand."

Saqqal sighed. "He means they might have left people up top to keep watch."

A man in a blue t-shirt and wearing some kind of ID badge around his neck approached and began asking what they were doing. Kruger lowered his binoculars and flashed his submachine gun at the man. "Fuck off."

The man saw the weapon and after looking up and seeing the other men he staggered backwards, almost tripping over one of the low walls running along the cultivation terraces.

"He'll call the police," Jawad said.

"Or army," Saqqal added.

Kruger was unmoved. "And even by chopper it will take them forever and a day to get here. We'll be in and out by then. By the time they turn up the only trace of us they'll find is the corpses of the bastard ECHO team."

Saqqal smiled with satisfaction, while Jawad shifted awkwardly on his feet. Behind them, Rajavi grabbed Balta by the collar and dragged him away from the helicopter.

Kruger stared at the ECHO team's chopper parked on the plaza and scowled. "Let's get this on."

CHAPTER TWENTY-ONE

Lea threw the mask up and watched with baited breath as Hawke fitted the Mask of Inti into the recess at the top of the pyramid. They all watched in the damp silence for a few seconds but nothing happened.

"Outstanding," Scarlet said. "I've had more excitement opening a packet of peanuts."

Then Hawke's eyes lit up "Wait!"

"What is it?" Lea asked.

"Look!"

The top section of the pyramid began to shake slightly, and then they heard a low, grinding noise before the capstone suddenly dropped an inch lower into the upper section. "It's opening the entrance to the pyramid," Reaper said.

Hawke nodded. "If we can get our hands under the gap this thing has just created we can lift it off."

Lea watched as Hawke and Reaper struggled with the stone lid of the pyramid. They were both red-faced with the effort of lifting the heavy block and grunting as they heaved it up and pushed it away to reveal a small gap.

"Can you see anything?" Lea said.

"Torch," Hawke said, holding his hand out.

Luis stepped up and gave him his flashlight.

Hawke switched it on and stepped up to the top of the pyramid once again, shining the light inside the small gap and then whistling with surprise.

"What do you see?" Reaper said.

"Yes, come on," said Scarlet. "Do tell."

Lea climbed up beside Hawke and peered down inside the gap. She gripped the stone lip of the pyramid as she followed Hawke's flashlight beam around the inside of the tomb. "Oh my!"

"Exactly what I thought," Hawke said.

They were looking at the inside of a tomb featuring the strange, seated remains of three dead bodies, mummified and each pointed so they were all facing the center. They were wrapped up in hand-woven textiles and placed neatly around them were various piles of ceramic ornaments, jewellery, weapons and tools for weaving.

"Why are they all sitting like that?" Lea asked, feeling a shiver go down her spine.

"Maybe they were waiting for a bus," Hawke said.

"No," Luis said, climbing up between them. "This is not the Inca way, but something much earlier."

But it was the sun that their dead, covered eyes were staring at that captivated all their attention. It was a large golden sun sculpture inlaid into the floor of the pyramid, and it was looking back at them with timeless eyes carved into the gold. It was two-dimensional, and rose only an inch or two above the floor, and all the way around it were sunbeams made from yet more gold. From what they could see, it looked like the center of the sun might be made from a separate piece of gold.

"I think we need a closer look," Hawke said. He rubbed his hands together and called out over his shoulder. "Grab me one of those ropes, will you Lexi?"

She handed him the rope and after securing it to the side of the pyramid he lowered it down inside the tomb. "Now then," he said, clambering over the edge. "No funny jokes involving putting the lid back on and locking me in, all right Cairo?"

"Me?" she said, pretended to be hurt. "Why would I do something like that?"

Hawke gave her a look and then slowly descended inside the pyramid tomb. Due to the angle of the wall as it moved out toward the base the rope dangled straight down without a wall beside it, and he knew that meant a tougher climb back up, but he continued to descend.

His boots crunched down on the tomb floor and kicked up a small cloud of dust. From above, the whole thing had looked eerie enough, but down here, face to face with the mummies on their own turf was downright creepy – especially the way they were all positioned to look down at the sun sculpture for eternity.

He shone the flashlight around the tomb and saw for the first time the murals on the upper walls of the pyramid. "Luis, I think you'd better take a look at this."

"Me? Go down there? Are you crazy?"

"Yes, yes, and no. Get a wriggle on."

"What is it, Joe?" Lea said.

"I don't know, but it looks like the same sort of stuff on the mask."

Luis climbed down the rope, but with a good deal more grunting and huffing than Hawke. Two-thirds of the way down he gave up and slid down, howling as the friction burned the palms of his hands. He hit the floor of the tomb a second later and began to run around in circles, cursing and blowing on his hands to try and cool them.

Hawke rolled his eyes and shone the flashlight in his face. "Are we ready now?"

"Si… I'm sorry. I haven't climbed a rope since gym class in school."

"What was that?" Scarlet called down. "Last week?"

"For your information, I am twenty-five years old!"

"Last week then…"

"Can we move on?" Lea said. "This place is creepy."

"You're telling me!" Hawke said. "I'm the one down here with the three amigos."

"Shit!" Scarlet said, shining her flashlight on the mummy in the north corner. "Did that one just move?"

"What?" Hawke said, taking a step back and raising his fists ready for a fight.

"Oh, sorry," she said. "I was just making up a load of bullshit for a laugh."

"Christ, Cairo!" Hawke said. "I'll get you back for that."

"Don't make promises you can't keep, darling."

Hawke shook his head and sighed, and then made his way inside the triangle formed by the three mummies to get closer to the golden sun in the center. He rubbed his hands together and began to turn the dial on the sun's face. When it had moved ninety degrees he heard a distinct, deep clunking sound and felt something give beneath the dial. "Looks like we're in business," he said under his breath.

He pulled on the grooves either side of the dial. Countless centuries had cemented it in place and the resistance was strong, but a few more tugs and it made another metallic *clunk* sound before coming away in his hands. He placed it down on the dusty floor and looked inside.

There was more pottery and jewellery, all of it bearing various depictions of the sun in the same style as the one they had just opened – but these were all just the support acts. In the center, wrapped in cloth and tied with string, had to be what they had been searching for.

He reached inside and pulled it out, laying it gently on the sun's face, and slowly unwrapped it. It was a thin, circular stone plaque covered in Incan carvings. For a moment the two men stared in wordless, breathless silence.

"Is this what I think it is, Luis?" Hawke said, but he already knew the answer thanks to the clear picture in the center of the plaque – mountains, suns, rivers… this was a map.

He nodded. "I am certain it must be," he said, his eyes widening with anticipation. "Just look at the image in the middle – this is without a doubt a map."

"Yes, but is it *the* map?"

Luis ran his fingers over the top of the three-dimensional relief map and nodded once again. "It must be – look where we found it!"

Hawke agreed. "All right – let's get it out of here before there's any trouble and then we can set about translating it when we're back in the light."

"What the hell is going on down there?" Scarlet called down. "Are the five of you playing strip poker or something?"

"Drole," Hawke shouted up. "Very drole. We're on our way back up."

"About time."

Hawke tried to help Luis but climbing ropes was a one-man venture, and after much huffing, puffing and whining and two false starts the young Colombian finally reached the top and was pulled over the edge by Reaper and Lexi. Hawke tied the plaque to the bottom of the rope and then climbed up a moment later. When he reached the top he pulled the rope up and brought the ancient plaque out of the pyramid tomb for the first time in centuries.

He laid it down on the side of the pyramid and they looked at it for a few moments, the light from their flashlights illuminating the small stone carvings on its surface and making it look like a picture of the moon with its mountains and craters.

"Is that it?" Scarlet said. "Looks like a dinner plate."

"This is no dinner plate," Luis said. "This is the Map of Paititi."

Lexi looked at him suspiciously. "How can you be so sure?"

"I can't be one hundred percent sure, I admit... but what else could it be? Besides, here – these are clearly the Andes, and this must surely by the jungle to the north. This here is Inti! He is marking the exact location of the Lost City! I admit it... I am converted. Now I believe!"

"If you say so," Scarlet said. "Looks like a pig's breakfast to me."

But Luis wasn't listening. He was just staring at the map with incredulity. "If we hadn't opened the tomb ourselves I would feel like someone is playing a joke on us. This map is almost identical to all the other maps that have ever existed but with one important difference – the depiction of Inti is on the other side of the mountains on this map... on the eastern slopes, not the western side. This proves once and for all the Lost City is not Vilcabamba!"

"Hang on," Scarlet said, chewing on some more coca leaves she'd found. "Do you mean that it's just a straight-forward sodding map and we don't have to decode, translate or otherwise bugger about with it?"

"Looks that way," Hawke said, taking the map from Luis. "I see what you mean about old Inti being on the other side of the mountains – and it looks like it's very specific as well. He's standing right on top of a mountain beside a tributary of the Amazon. I think we can definitely use this map to find Paititi!"

He shone his flashlight over the outer chamber once again. "Time to get out of here I think."

"Wait – what was that noise?" Lexi said.

Reaper shrugged his shoulders. "The wind."

"No – I heard it too," Lea said.

And then the battle started.

CHAPTER TWENTY-TWO

In the darkness of Inti's tomb, the muzzle flashes of Kruger's small army illuminated the walls as they marched on the much smaller ECHO team. "Get those bastards!" Kruger yelled. "I want that damned map and the man who brings it to me gets a bigger cut."

The deafening sound of the skirmish rang out in the enclosed space as bullets traced and criss-crossed in every direction. Chunks of plaster tumbled out of the support beams and Hawke watched with increasing unease as the granite blocks in the ceiling came under fire.

"If those clowns detonate a grenade in here we're all getting flushed out in a hurry."

Corzo screamed with depraved joy as he unloaded an entire magazine in five seconds, the bullets spitting out of the muzzle and ripping into the masonry over Hawke's head.

"Kill them all!" Saqqal yelled. "And get that damned map!"

Rajavi stormed forward and unsheathed a savage pesh-kabz knife. From Iran, the pesh-kabz blade was designed by ancient Persians and Afghans to tear into chainmail armour. Traditionally a thrusting blade, its length and width meant it could be used almost as a short sword in the right hands. Judging by how Rajavi was manipulating it, his were the right hands.

The massive Iranian strongman waved the pesh-kabz in Hawke's face and beckoned him to come forward. In response, Hawke unsheathed his kukri and took a step toward him. The blade of the savage kukri flashed in the low light. It was a one-handed killing machine carried by Gurkhas for centuries and had gotten Hawke out of many tight situations.

The other man's response was instant, lunging forward with the pesh-kabz. He slashed it in Hawke's face, but the SBS man was ready and took a step back, swinging his head to the left at the same time.

Hawke's opponent wasn't easily deterred and upon Saqqal's orders he moved in closer to the Englishman and struck out again with the blade. Hawke dodged the second attack and this time brought up the kukri blade in a sweeping arc which slashed through Rajavi's arm from the cho or notch at the bolster all the way to the tip of the blade.

The Iranian screamed in pain at the wound which the weight and width of the blade had ensured went all the way to the bone. He dropped his knife and staggered back. Blood poured down his arm in spirals and ran off his elbow.

Hawke struck like a cobra, lunging forward and seizing the advantage. When he reached the man he raised the heavy blade and brought the handle down on his head hard, striking his skull with the buttcap of the knife. Anyone else would have been knocked out in a flash, but Rajavi was like a man of steel. With his arm bleeding wildly, he shook off the head strike and lashed out at Hawke, knocking him several yards across the chamber floor.

Chaos reigned in the chamber now and they were all engaged in hand to hand fights for their own survival. Lexi was on a high ridge above the entrance to the chamber fighting a CGF rebel while Lea, Scarlet and Ryan were taking their frustrations out on rebels closer to the pyramid. Luis was keeping back, but now the young Colombian academic called out as Saqqal approached him and raised a blade to his face. "Help!"

From out of nowhere, a grenade blasted Luis and Saqqal off their feet and slammed them against the side of the pyramid where Luis narrowly avoided cracking his skull on the granite side. As he flew through the air like a Frisbee, he released the map and it crashed into the dusty floor with a smack.

Saqqal's eyes lit up like they were on fire. "There it is!"

Luis scrambled forward to retrieve the ancient map and snatched it up in his hands, but now Saqqal grabbed his knife and approached him once again while all around them the fight raged on.

"Give me the stone, or I will kill you."

"Help!"

"No one can hear you... they are all fighting for their lives. How will you defend your own life?" He flicked his fingers to indicate that Luis should hand over the stone. "One more chance."

Across the chamber, Reaper was working his legionnaire magic on Corzo, pummelling him so hard in the stomach he nearly lost his balance. The Colombian rebel was harder than he looked and took the blows without a reaction and then fought back with a vicious right hook which knocked Reaper back a few steps and gave his opponent the time he needed to regain his strength and get ready for another attack.

Both men were working hard to get the better of the other, but neither was giving any quarter as the fight progressed from fists to knives. Hawke watched now as the Frenchman struggled against the much younger man. Corzo was trying to bring his knife up into the bottom of Reaper's ribcage, and the only thing stopping it was the last few ounces of strength the former legionnaire could muster.

His contorted face dripped with sweat as he grunted with the effort of deflecting the Colombian's blade, but Hawke saw it was slowly inching its way closer to his stomach. The strain on his eyes was clear enough as they blinked like a madman's with each inch he edged the blade closer to Reaper's ribcage. Corzo used his other hand to smash Reaper's blade to the floor and he kicked it away into the shadows.

Slowly the blade got closer, and Hawke could see his friend was in trouble. He threw the kukri and struck Corzo with the juro, or peak of the blade. The Colombian grunted with pain and shock and stumbled back a few steps, reaching up to feel the gash on his head.

"Merci bien, mon ami," Reaper said.

"No problem, Reap."

He watched as Corzo suddenly retreated and saw Rajavi was doing the same. "They're pulling out!" he said.

"Why?" Reaper said.

Hawke frowned "They must have the....*oh no!*" He ran over to where he had left Luis and then he saw it. The young man was dead, murdered by Ziad Saqqal and the stone map wrenched out of his hands.

Lea ran over to him, panting with the effort of the fight. "What is it, Joe? Oh God!"

"They killed him," Hawke said, his voice a low whisper. "He was trying to keep the map from them, and Saqqal murdered him for it." He took off his jacket and gently rested it over Luis's body.

They were broken from their shock by the sound of submachine gunfire. Hawke squinted to protect his eyes as wave after wave of bullets blasted the hell out of their corner of the tomb. Behind them from the safety of the entrance tunnel, the Syrian commander had ordered the rebels to stay and finish them off.

In the tunnel behind the men, Hawke could see the heads of Ziad Saqqal, Dirk Kruger, Jawad, Rajavi and Corzo as they bobbed up and down on their way out of the underground complex.

In the new front line created by the rebels, one of the men was now walking toward them with an M60 in his hands and preparing to fire on them.

"We have to get that map back!" he yelled.

"You might have noticed we're sort of occupied right now," Scarlet said. She held her handgun at arm's length and rested the weapon on the edge of the pyramid as she took aim. Moments later three sharp shots found their way home, dropping the rebel playing Platoon with the M60. He hit the dirt like a snake and crawled for cover, badly wounded, but he still had the weapon.

And then someone yelled from above. "Drop it like it's hot, motherfucker!"

Hawke looked up to see Lexi Zhang. She was still on the ridge above the entrance, and having disposed of her opponent she was now aiming her gun at the man with the M60 below her.

The man's eyes flicked nervously from Lexi to Hawke. *Drop the gun or not drop the gun...* He moved forward to put the gun on the floor, but hesitated for a second before starting to rise again.

And he was dead a second later, slamming face first into the dirt. Above him on the ridge Lexi's smoking pistol was the only clue as to what had happened.

They all turned to look at her. "He was going to shoot," she said. "I saw it in his eyes. Easier to read than a Mr Man book."

"I'm glad you're on my side," Reaper said.

135

"And who says I'm on your side, Reap?"

He laughed. "You never give anything away and you never have done."

"You really *do* know me, Vincent!" she said, blowing him a kiss.

She turned to walk back down to the main chamber when a rebel leaped from the shadows behind her and drew his gun.

She tried to turn her gun on him but there was no room on the narrow ledge.

He raised his weapon and prepared to fire.

She knew she had only one chance, and so she seized it.

Leaping from the ridge she tumbled over the edge and began to fall to the rocky floor far below.

The rebel was now aiming his gun at her, determined to kill her with a bullet before she hit the dirt.

Hawke aimed and threw the kukri as fast as he could. It spun through the air in a series of flashes until striking the man. The chunky blade buried itself in the man's throat and sent him staggering off the ledge a second after Lexi.

Hawke put his hands out to catch her, taking a step forward as she fell toward him. She landed with a crash in his arms and looked up at him. "My hero."

"You, my friend," Hawke said, taking a step back again so the man crashed into the dirt at his boots, "...are welcome anytime."

He lowered her to the ground and pulled the kukri from the man's neck, wiping the blade clean on his jacket.

"I'll keep that in mind," she said with a wink.

"Not that sort of welcome, Lexi."

"Oh..."

They looked up to see Reaper running over to them. "They're lining the tunnel with explosives!"

Before anyone could react, a tremendous explosion roared out in the tunnel and in the chamber. They watched in horror as the water from the aquifer flooded down into the tunnel and began to fill it up.

Scarlet sighed. "Oh, happy, joyful day…"

"Saqqal's an idiot," Hawke said.

Lea looked at him. "Eh?"

"The tunnel leading up from the hole in the mountain to this chamber was uphill. All the water from that aquifer is going to flow down to the outside of the tunnel."

"Are you sure?"

"It's called gravity," Ryan said sullenly.

"Anyone here ever enjoy going on water slides?"

They all turned to look at him, but only Reaper grinned.

Hawke led them into the tunnel to the location of the explosion. The noise of the rushing water was deafening, but he was right. The water from the citadel's aquifer was flowing at great pressure through the hole created by Saqqal's detonation, but gravity was redirecting it straight down the incline toward the hole they had discovered under the rock on the surface.

"Deep breath everyone," Hawke said. "And arms crossed over the body."

With that he leaped into the jet and disappeared into the high-pressure white water.

Lea leaped next, and immediately regretted her decision. That lying, bullshitting, sneaky, good-for-nothing, optimistic son-of-a-bitch had definitely not been on any of the water slides she'd been on and that was for keeps. The water was freezing cold for one thing, and next it was moving about ten times faster than any sodding slide.

It spat her out at the other end like a champagne cork and after siding all over the now soaked grass of the clearing she came to a stop and gasped for air as she pulled her hair out of her face. "You bastard!" she said, and scrambled clear of the water jet.

The torrent now spat Reaper out.

"What?" Hawke was standing on the granite slab they'd blown up to make the entrance. He was shielding his eyes and watching Saqqal and Kruger as they were jogging back to their choppers. "They're nearly at the top... damn it."

Lexi now fired out and skidded to a halt a second before Ryan.

"What do you mean, *what?*"

Now Scarlet came through, screaming with excitement.

Hawke turned to Lea. "Eh? You're really wet by the way."

She felt the fury rising. "I'm really wet? Of course I'm really freaking wet, you fool!" She walked up to him and got in his face. "That wasn't anything like a pissing waterslide! That was a freaking torpedo tube!"

"Ah yes," he said with a grin. "But if I'd told you that none of you would have followed me."

She leaned forward and kissed him on the lips. "You crazy, mad bastard."

Breathless and exhausted, they gathered together and began to jog up the hill toward the citadel. Moments later they heard a chopper's engine starting up.

"We have to hurry," Lea said. "Or they're gone – and they've got the sodding map stone."

CHAPTER TWENTY-THREE

At the top of the hill, the first thing Hawke saw was smoke billowing from their Eurocopter. Saqqal or Kruger had ordered their men to destroy it and they had obeyed. There was no way they were flying anywhere in that thing.

Then they caught sight of the enemy. Kruger was in the pilot's seat and increasing power to the chopper while Saqqal, Jawad, Rajavi, Corzo and a couple of surviving rebels were clambering inside and belting up. To the east a Mi-171 chopper with Peruvian Army markings was landing in the ancient cultivation terraces and armed soldiers were jumping out. Behind it, a small two-seater Bell 47 was landing beyond the House of the Guardians. Inside were a pilot and a man with a news camera.

"That's all we need," Lea said. "Bloody news crew."

Hawke frowned. "They're the least of our worries."

The surviving rebels took up a defensive position behind the city gate and opened fire on the soldiers. The Peruvians tried to scatter for cover but the surprise attack was too deadly and they were all wiped out in seconds. The pilot began to lift the chopper but a rebel fired through the windshield and took him out before the machine was ten inches above the ground. The helicopter crashed back down to earth, its rotors still whirring.

The ECHO team sprinted forward but couldn't stop the rebels who were now piling inside the Venom and lifting up into the air behind Kruger.

Hawke turned to Reaper. "You still know how to fly a chopper?"

The Frenchman peered over at the Mi-171 and nodded. "Mais, oui…"

"Right, then let's do this. I'll take the journos' Bell and go after the rebels, you take the army chopper and get Kruger."

They divided into two teams, with Hawke and Scarlet running to the Bell while Reaper led the rest of the team to the Mi-171.

Hawke and Scarlet approached the Bell. The pilot was still inside, but the engine was off and the rotors now perfectly still. The man with the news camera was trying to zoom in on the burning Eurocopter in the Main Square, but Scarlet kept getting in his way.

"Move!" he said in English, and then in Spanish: "Damned tourists!"

The boot was fast, and as accurate as ever. A second later Scarlet was removing the camera from the hands of the howling newsman and hurling it over the sheer drop beyond the City Gate.

The former SBS man opened the chopper's door, unbuckled the pilot's belt and dragged him out of the machine in less than ten seconds. He told the pilot to stay down as he clambered in, but while Scarlet was joining him and buckling up both the pilot and the newsman scuttled away and started yelling for someone to call the police.

The former SBS man had piloted many choppers in his time, the last time being when he had evacuated the team from the missing Temple of Huitzilopochtli in the Lacandon Jungle, but this thing barely looked airworthy.

He consoled himself with the fact the news crew had gotten it up here in the first place and immediately began the starting procedures while Scarlet checked the weapons were ready to go and slung an ammo belt over her shoulder.

"Are you dressing up for me?" he asked with a grin.

"Shut up and fly, Josiah."

A great idea, he thought, and glanced out the window to make sure the main rotor was untied. He knew it was, because it had just landed here but it was a habit drilled into him years ago and now unshakeable, like checking the fuel caps were secured.

He scanned the panel: avionics off, strobe on and then he reached down and pushed the fuel shut-off in before checking the hydraulic boost switch was off.

"Can't you go any faster?"

"Cairo, this isn't the Sweeney and we're not in a Ford Granada. You don't just jump in one of these things and magic it into the air. It's not Hollywood."

She looked him up and down. "You don't have to tell me that, darling. You'd look more like Matt Damon if this was Hollywood."

"What the hell is that supposed to mean?"

"When was the last time you went to the gym?"

"How the hell should... listen, I've got work to do so put your seatbelt on and can it."

Hawke turned away from Scarlet with a look of incredulity before loosening the friction on the cyclic and the collective and made sure the anti-torque pedals and cyclic were all free and unrestricted.

"They're getting away, Joe!" she said, the frustration rising in her voice. "They'll be in shagging Paititi before you get this thing off the ground."

Hawke wiped the sweat from his face and sighed as if he were dealing with a child. "Again… if you would just kindly shut your mouth I'll be much quicker."

Hawke checked the friction was set on the throttle and then replaced the friction and returned the controls to neutral, set carb heat to cold and made sure the comms were on. Then he turned the magnetos on and primed the engine by twisting the throttle and then set it for start.

"They're almost out of sight! Christ almighty!"

"It's such a shame I won't be able to hear a word you say when the engine's on."

With that he turned the ignition key and watched carefully as the rotor engine's RPMs began to rise. The ageing chopper began to vibrate as the engine picked up speed and the rotors started whirring faster and faster until they were a blur.

Hawke switched on the radio and waited until the revs passed thirty and then the familiar *whomp whomp whomp* sound of the rotors began. A final check on the magnetos and the carb temp and then he raised the collective. Scarlet made a big deal about things with fake applause when the Bell finally lifted off the ground but she piped down when a strong westerly blew the small chopper hard to the starboard and Hawke had to fight to bring her level again as they ascended.

He smirked as she settled down in her seat, and they couldn't help but marvel as they looked down at the incredible view of Machu Picchu afforded to them by the plexiglass bubble cockpit on the Bell 47. Looking past his feet on the rudders, the amazing fifteenth century citadel of the Incas stretched out in a blaze of gold and green as the sun lit its intricate terraces and walls.

A second later it was gone as he increased power on the collective and gently pushed the cyclic forward. Ahead of them, the rebels were making good progress along the Sacred Valley. They tore over the Urubamba River and then pulled up sharply to fly over the top of the next range.

Hawke gave chase, and his superior piloting skills allowed him to close the gap before they too crossed the next range and saw the Andes fading into the jungles of northern Cusco Province.

Scarlet peered through her side of the bubble. "Get lost out here and you're more fucked than the ship's cat."

"Oh, *really*," he said in disgust. "I thought you were supposed to be a bloody aristocrat or something?"

"Me? Hardly, darling. Common as muck."

But she had a point. Ahead of them, the rebels' chopper looked ridiculously small as it hung in the air above the unimaginably vast landscape, but Hawke powered forward without fear.

The rebels suddenly lunged down toward the valley and began turning sharply to the right.

"Looks like the bastards don't like being chased," Scarlet said.

Hawked lowered the collective, pushing the Bell into the same diving pattern and making the same turn. "Have to stay on their tail or they get the advantage."

"Shouldn't you be levelling off around now?" Scarlet said, nervously eyeing the Urubamba River as it rushed up towards them.

"You're not scared are you, Cairo?" he said.

"Of course not," she said not too convincingly.

Just as he heard her gasp through his headphones he gently raised the collective and levelled off, also completing the turn at the same time. The rebels' more powerful helicopter was still in front of them.

Ahead of them they watched as a goon in black began to climb halfway out the rear window.

"They're firing!" Scarlet yelled.

"Yes, thank you, Cairo," Hawke said. "For a moment I wondered if he was leaning out to invite us to Kruger's next birthday bash, but now I can see I was wrong."

"Tit," she said in a whisper, but it was clear enough through the headphones.

He looked at her.

"What?" she said.

"Well, are you going to shoot back, or what?"

"Oh, yeah. Natch."

She slid back her window and they were instantly buffeted by the wind, but she didn't flinch as she pulled out a Glock and smacked a fresh round into the grip. "Always a pleasure to give back what you receive."

And with that she began firing, but so did the other guy. Hawke swerved the chopper from port to starboard and back again to avoid being hit, but he knew he was also reducing Scarlet's chance of hitting the rebels.

The other chopper slowed and pulled alongside them and the rear portside door slid open to reveal a rebel staring back at them. In his hands was a handheld M320 grenade launcher. He fired a round at their Bell and it shot through the air toward them. He had timed it wrong, and it exploded twenty yards short, blasting the Bell over to port but no more pain than a small correction on the cyclic which Hawke made with a gentle touch, and then he raised the collective to gain elevation.

The Venom followed suit, pulling up and maintaining the same altitude as their much smaller Bell 47. The rebel fired another round, and it tore through the mountain air en route to the Bell. Hawke pulled hard to port and descended but this time the rebel had improved his aim and the explosion was much closer, blasting the Bell much harder to port and almost tipping her over.

The Venom pulled around and followed them down as they raced toward the bottom of the ravine.

Hawke saw the rocks racing up toward them but didn't raise the collective. "When I was leaving the SBS I thought about working as a pilot doing helicopter tourist rides."

"I think security guard was a better choice," Scarlet said, eyes widening as the rocks raced closer. The Urubamba River was now so close she could make out the reeds being pulled along by the current. "And now might be the time to get us out of this dive."

"Not yet."

She made no reply but gripped the sides of the seat.

And then Hawke lifted the collective and scooped the tiny Bell out of the dive before levelling her off less than twenty feet above the Urubamba. "A spot of low-level flying is in order."

"You trained for that, right?"

He glanced at her. "Er, yeah…"

"What does that mean?"

"It means no."

She shook her head as she reloaded her Glock. "Bloody fantastic, Hawke."

"There has to be a first time for everything," he replied. "You'll know that when you make your first funny joke."

She flicked her eyes at him but said nothing. She loosened her belt and turned in her seat. She opened the small window and leaned her head out. "Bastards right on our six o'clock, Josiah."

Hawke lowered the Bell to ten feet. They were so low now the rotorwash was flicking up spray from the

Urubamba as they flashed over the top of it, following its meanders with the mountains high on either side of them.

Scarlet fired at the Venom, striking the cockpit windshield and puncturing bullets in a neat line across it. The rebels swerved the larger helicopter to starboard and shifted her out of Scarlet's sights. "Balls... he's gone again."

With the sound of their rotors echoing off the sides of the mountains rising high above them on all sides, Hawke weaved the chopper deftly around the twists and turns of the river in a bid to evade more rounds from their grenade launcher but it was too late and the next thing he knew there was a massive explosion in front of the chopper.

The rebels had fired a grenade over the top of them and now Hawke had no choice but to fly right through the middle of the fireball as it burned out in the air ahead of them.

"Holy shit!" Scarlet said.

"Seconded!"

For a couple of seconds they were surrounded by the fireball, their vision cut off by a raging cloud of flames all around the Perspex bubble cockpit, but then they were through and back in the clear air.

"They *really* do not like you," Scarlet said.

"Eh? It's you they want!"

Hawke saw a narrow pass almost hidden on the right, tucked in behind the western ridge of a mountain, and without warning he banked hard to starboard and left the river behind.

Scarlet screamed and gripped the grab handle as they tipped over on their side. As Hawke raised the collective she felt the extra Gs for a few seconds and watched through Hawke's window as they skimmed the canopy of the rainforest on the river's east bank. "I'm going to say no thanks to your tourist idea."

He smiled but made no reply as he focussed on levelling the chopper and zooming into the narrower ravine. "How are our friends?"

Scarlet looked out her window and sighed. "Bastards sticking to us like glue."

"The goon?"

"He's leaning out for another go."

She aimed her gun and fired at the rebel, striking the port skid of the chopper and forcing him back inside. "We're going to need to bring this situation to an end, Josiah. I'm down to my last three rounds."

"I think I see our way out up ahead."

She turned in her seat and almost screamed. Racing up to meet them was a large waterfall, maybe two hundred feet high. "Please tell me you're not going to do what I think you're going to do."

"Sorry... no can do."

Hawke was not a gambling man, but now he was gambling that the Venom couldn't see past the Bell because of the heavy canopy above the tributary, and so the waterfall would make a nasty surprise... a nasty *unavoidable* surprise if he could just hold his nerve for long enough.

He tightened his grip on the cyclic and collective and slowed his breathing as the waterfall grew ever bigger ahead of them. It was so close now they could both make out the slabs of granite through the white water as it rushed over the upstream retreats of the falls and tumbled over the overhang on its way down into the Urubamba's tributary.

"Are you sure this is a good idea, Joe?"

147

"Of course I'm bloody not!" he said, flicking her a nervous glance. "I find in situations like this it's usually better not to think."

"Oh, how very reassuring to hear your pilot say that."

Hawke raised the collective, altering the angle of the main rotor blades and lifting the chopper into a climb. At the same time he pushed his right foot on the rudder and changed the angle of the tail rotors to move the chopper to the right. The Bell shot up away from the top of the waterfall and zoomed off to the right, clipping the leaves on the top of the canopy for a second before he levelled the machine up.

Behind them, the Venom had no time to react and a second later it smashed into the hard rock at the top of the waterfall behind the overhang. It exploded into a massive fireball and sprayed gas-fuelled flames all over the rainforest canopy.

Scarlet hung out her window and yelled with glee as the wrecked chopper dropped like a dead fly into the plunge pool and disappeared under the foam and spray of the falling water. "Not confident Kruger's getting his deposit back on the Venom."

Hawke grinned. "I take it that my little plan worked?"

"*This* time, you total idiot, you got lucky."

"And I thought Dirk was the lucky one..."

Hawke lifted the chopper away from the canopy and turned it south toward Machu Picchu.

CHAPTER TWENTY-FOUR

Vincent Reno was starting to think he was getting too old for this line of work. True, he found strength by recalling his French Foreign Legion days, but those days were a long way behind him now. Some argued you never really stopped being a legionnaire, but that wasn't true for him.

When he left the hardened ranks of the legion, he took his training and experience into Francophone Africa where he worked as an independent mercenary. After that he was the proverbial lost soul, drifting around from odd job to odd job and trying to stay on the straight and narrow to give his kids a decent life in the south of France.

Then his life took a radical change of direction when his old friend Scarlet Sloane had called him one day and drawn him into the Poseidon mission. Then, things had changed in a big way. He'd learned things about a world he thought he knew... things that had shocked him to his core, but, he thought with a Gallic shrug, nothing Vincent Reno couldn't handle.

He wasn't scared by what they had learned in Atlantis and the Seastead. If anything, it had given him a new lease of life. If it was true, and they really were facing a corrupt cabal of people who possessed the power of immortality, then he wanted to get to the bottom of it. If what they had learned was real, then the Athanatoi and its various chapters were like a crust of scum keeping the rest of humanity in eternal darkness and ignorance.

Smashing that crust and letting the daylight flow in was his kind of day job.

More than that, breaking through their ranks and getting to their dark heart promised more than simply ending their grip on global power and understanding how they worked their magic with the elixir. It also meant discovering something they had kept behind a veil for millennia... something about the origins of humanity that his heart told his head he had to know, for himself, his wife, his twin boys and everyone else in the world.

He respectfully removed the dead pilot from the Mi-171 and fired up the engine as the others climbed in, put on their helmets and buckled up. He raised the collective to ascend the chopper into a hover above the ruins of the ancient citadel. Immediately the main rotor started vibrating and they began to lose altitude.

"What's going on?" Lea asked.

Vincent noticed the sink rate increase and the vibration on the main rotors get worse. "It's called a vortex ring state," the Frenchman replied. "It's when the rotors are engulfed by an air vortex." As he spoke, he adjusted the cyclic and corrected the problem. "It's fine now."

"I don't think so!" Lexi yelled, pointing out the rear starboard window. Kruger's chopper had turned in the sky and was now flying toward them. It slowed to a hover above the citadel's ancient Prisoners' Area and that's when they saw the side door open.

"What the hell are they doing?" Lexi asked.

She got her answer when Mauricio Balta's dead body was thrown out into the wind. His clothes and hair flapped about in the downdraft as he tumbled out of sight in the ravine.

"Animals," Lea said.

"And they're not stopping there," Reaper said.

They looked to see Rajavi shoulder an RPG7 while Corzo loaded a rocket into it. "They're not playing games."

"Damn it!" Reaper said. "Thanks to the VRS we're too low!"

Rajavi hung outside the chopper and then a flash of smoke puffed out the back of the RPG launcher sending a rocket racing toward their helicopter. It left a trail of twisting white exhaust smoke drifting in a thin line above the citadel's cemetery.

"Flare!" Reaper yelled through the comms, and then swung the chopper around to face the missile, reducing their overall target area.

Lea instantly pulled the flare dispenser from under her seat and grabbed the latch on the window. She slid the window open, and fired a decoy flare out the portside.

Reaper tipped the chopper hard to the right, almost pulling her on her side as the rocket screeched past them and struck the countermeasure. They all felt the explosion as it blasted against the bottom of the chopper but Reaper used his experience to bring her level and true. "We need altitude!"

He pulled her up to the maximum climb rate of eight meters per second and swung her one-eighty out over the valley. A second ago they were fifty feet above Machu Picchu, but now they were hundreds of feet above the Urubamba River.

Reaper sighed with relief. "Thank those guys for me, will you Lexi?"

The Chinese assassin nodded. She slid open her window and began spraying the two-man RPG crew with gunfire, but Kruger was an excellent pilot and easily dodged the line of fire.

151

Reaper dropped the collective and made the chopper dive down the western slope of the mountain. Machu Picchu flashed past them and was gone in a second, replaced by the lush green of the rainforest. Lea screamed and reached out for the grab handle as the Frenchman brought the machine under control, his mind split four ways between the collective, the cyclic, the rudders and the control panel. At over one hundred and twenty miles per hour and racing through a narrow valley while trying to avoid incoming fire from Kruger's chopper, it took every ounce of his concentration.

"Are you sure you know what you're doing?" Ryan said.

"Bien sûr," Reaper replied. "The last time I flew one of these the instructor said I was one of his best students."

Lexi gasped. "The last time you flew a helicopter was with an *instructor?*"

He nodded.

"So you're not qualified?"

He shook his head. "Sadly, no."

"Oh, shit!"

"Ah," Reaper said, smiling at the memory. "1984 was a great year."

Ryan and Lexi shared a horrified glance. "1984?"

"Mais, oui."

"So let me get this straight," Lea said. "You're not qualified to fly a helicopter and the last time you flew one was before any of us was born?"

Reaper gave his famous Gallic shrug. "You really know how to make a guy feel old, you know that?"

He plunged the chopper into another dive. No one in the chopper could believe what they had just heard, but Lexi moved first and begun to load her gun.

"I don't think you can hit Kruger from this range," Ryan said.

"It's not for Kruger," she said coldly. "If Monsieur Reaper loses control of this thing I'm going out with a bullet, not in a burning heap of twisted metal. Would you like me to extend the same courtesy to you?"

Ryan swallowed hard and widened his eyes as he stared at the muzzle of her gun. "No thanks, you're all right."

Kruger's chopper was directly behind them now, and dived down in pursuit of them as they opened fire once again. Rajavi was leaning out the sliding door with one hand looped around the handle while he fired his submachine gun with the other hand. Wild sprays of bullets traced all over the ECHO chopper as Reaper swung the cyclic from side to side to dodge the flying rounds. If they struck the gas tank they would be a fireball half a second later, and then nothing but burning debris raining down into the jungle canopy below.

Ahead of them the Urubamba River was racing up into their faces at a terrifying rate of knots. The Frenchman responded with a whispered curse and then a hefty pull back on the collective.

He was late and the chopper's skids broke the surface of the river and ripped through the rushing torrent, spraying water up on both sides of the helicopter. For a second the chopper was destabilized and Reaper pushed his left boot down hard on the rudder to avoid tipping over and losing his lift.

They spun around like a speeding car on a greasy skid pan and a second later it was facing the opposite direction.

Kruger was now bearing down on them, so close that an impact was almost inevitable, but he pulled up on the collective and shot over the top of them at high speed.

Its skids barely missed the speeding rotors of the ECHO helicopter, but then it was clear.

Reaper was still trying to bring their helicopter under control and stop the spin, which he did by careful use of the rudders and then pushed forward on the cyclic stick to get his forward momentum back. He lifted the collective and they shot up into the air again, leaving the rushing Urubamba far below them.

"That was thirty seconds I hope I never have to repeat," Lea said.

"What are you talking about!" Lexi said. "It was great!"

Lea turned in her seat and gave her a sideways glance. "If you say so."

"I do! What do you think, Ryan?"

"I think I need to change my underwear."

Reaper was now following Kruger and rising up behind him like an Exocet missile. "Now the bastards are running from us."

Lea opened her window and opened fire with her handgun, and from where they were sitting they could see her bullets striking the rear of the chopper's main body.

Kruger responded in a heartbeat, spinning around to the right and ascending in order to fly over the top of a series of drumlins before climbing more sharply and reaching a smooth plateau.

Reaper pursued, and the two choppers were now racing in the Peruvian sunshine across the rocky scree-covered plateau on their way to a higher ridgeline.

Lea fired again but this time she missed and now she was out of bullets. She cursed and shook her head, but Lexi took over. Trying to bring a helicopter down with a handgun was a long shot at the best of times but at this speed it was almost impossible.

Lexi tried her best but she too was out of bullets in seconds and then the game was almost over. When Kruger flew up into the clouds and disappeared out of sight, the game was completely over.

"We can still find them!" Lea said.

Reaper shook his head. "Not now... not in these clouds. Not without any weapons. We're out of luck."

"So what now?" Lexi said, the frustration clear in her voice.

"Now we find Joe and Scarlet."

CHAPTER TWENTY-FIVE

Hawke tapped the fuel gauge and sighed. The problem with these small helicopters is they had small fuel tanks, and this one wasn't full to start with. He looked out into the world's biggest jungle and surveyed an empty horizon with concern.

"What is it?" Scarlet asked, noticing him tap the gauge once again.

"Nothing we can do anything about, put it that way."

"Oh, how very reassuring," she said. "Don't ever train to be a commercial airline pilot, for fuck's sake."

"Don't worry – I won't," he said.

And then the radio crackled. "What's up?"

It was Reaper's voice, calling over the comms from the other chopper. They had coordinated their positions over the radio and were now flying side by side.

"Just a little low on fuel," Hawke said. "Nothing serious."

"How low, Joe?"

Lea's voice now, and she didn't sound impressed with the nonchalant way he had reported the fuel situation.

"We're fine, but we might need a ride home with you guys if that's okay."

"Always happy to give Scarlet a ride," Reaper replied.

"In your dreams, Vincent," came the crackly reply.

Hawke smiled as the banter unfolded over the comms between the two helicopters. They were thundering their way from Machu Picchu to the location where they all hoped they would find Paititi, the Lost City of the Incas, and keeping their spirits up was essential to any successful mission.

"You're sure you can remember the location, mate?"

No response from the other chopper.

"Ryan?"

"Yeah, no problem."

"Good," Hawke said. "We need to send the coordinates to Lund in case there's trouble."

"You're sure, aren't you, Ry?" Lea said. "Cause this ain't the sort of place we want to get lost."

"I said I could remember it," he snapped.

Hawke left it there. He knew Saqqal and Kruger had a head start on them, but there was no doubt in his heart at all that his friends in the ECHO team wouldn't be able to turn it around to their own advantage. They had never failed on a mission yet and they weren't about to start now.... except maybe the Seastead.

The thought rose in his mind like a ghost drifting through a misty graveyard. Had they failed at the Seastead? Yes, maybe they had, he thought. They had allowed the Oracle to flee into the storm and take the Mictlan idol with him, and if that wasn't bad enough they had let Kruger slip away with Ryan as a hostage as well. He was safe now but it could have ended with his death, just like it did for Maria.

He wished he could shake the thought out of his head forever, but that would mean forgetting about her altogether.

Scarlet leaned forward in her seat and switched off the radio so their conversation was private. "You're thinking about Maria?"

He turned to face her, startled. "Yes... how did you know?"

"You looked so angry all of a sudden. I know you, Joe."

Hawke didn't know how to answer. Like with Sophie and Olivia, he held himself personally responsible for Maria's death. Eden might be the head of the ECHO team, but Hawke was the man in charge in the field and he felt the pressure of it more with every mission.

Now he had to move Maria into the growing list of men and women who had died under his command, and it was starting to get to him. He found himself increasingly uncertain if he wanted to lead the team, just at exactly the same time as Eden had been knocked out of the game and landed in hospital with a life-threatening injury. If there was a way for him to fight through all of this and find any peace, then he didn't know how to do it.

All he knew how to do was push thoughts like this aside and focus on the task at hand. There was no strategic success without tactical success. The ghost of a smile played on his cut lips as he recalled his training back in the marines. But it worked, and now his head was full of Ziad Saqqal, Dirk Kruger and the peculiar Rajavi. They didn't have much to go on, but they never needed much, and this was one mission that everyone was going to survive.

He felt Scarlet glaring at him and turned to see her smiling. She looked good when she smiled, but it happened so rarely that he barely recognized her.

"What?"

"You're all right for a stupid bastard, did you know that?"

"Thanks, I think…"

"Welcome."

"How's Jack?"

"Camo? He can survive being ridden hard and put away wet, if that's what you mean."

"Not *exactly* what I was getting at."

"If you're referring to the boring stuff, then yes… I think we could have a future. He's nowhere near as annoying as you."

"I'm so pleased for you," he said. "Still thinking about quitting?"

"If I had half a chance to think about it, I might," she said, lighting a cigarette. She blew the smoke out. Hawke coughed and opened the window an inch.

"You don't mind?" she said, already on her third drag.

"No, just thinking about the drag on the chopper."

"Problem is," she said, totally ignoring the point, "I never seem to get that chance. We finish a mission, go back to the island, have a shower and then there's another sodding crisis."

"I'm starting to understand that little feature of ECHO life. It's like being trapped in a revolving door."

"Exactly, darling. Poor Jack doesn't understand." She turned to face Hawke again. "He asked me to quit ECHO, did you know that?"

"Really?"

"Yeah. Says we're too old to be fighting bad guys and that we should put our heads together and find somewhere nice to retire."

"And what did you say?"

She flicked the half-smoked cigarette out the window. "I said he's a cheeky shit and I'm not that old."

"About the retirement thing."

"Ah – well… I didn't know what to say."

With the bright Peruvian sunshine beaming into the cockpit, she folded her arms, yawned and closed her eyes. "Wake me when we get there."

"You got it."

"That's presuming Ryan knows where the sodding place is, of course."

Yes, Hawke thought... *that's presuming Ryan knows where the sodding place is.*

CHAPTER TWENTY-SIX

Tiger kept his songbirds in little bamboo cages. The cages hung from a Chinese plum tree in the corner of his garden. Some preferred teak cages, but this was too showy for Tiger. Tiger liked to keep things simple. *A bird does not sing because it has an answer,* he thought, *but because it has a song.*

He cocked his head almost robotically as he cooed at a Sichuan Bush Warbler and tapped his forefinger on the bamboo bars. He sighed and sat back on his bench, surveying his garden. It was a modest affair in Beijing's Shunyi District. Here in the northeast quarters he was happy enough in his little villa and the pollution was much lower than further in the city. That was important to him, and especially important to his songbirds.

Over his wall he heard some people arguing about prices in the flower market. This was all normal enough and rarely disrupted his contemplation as he sat in his beloved Chinese garden. It was here where he did his most precious thinking, among the bamboo, plums and pear trees. Last year he had planted a pomegranate tree but it had failed to shoot. Another crease to iron out, but now he had a job to do.

Zhang Xiaoli was a problem, but perhaps Zhou Yang was thinking more of his reputation than any security risks. He had worked with Xiaoli several times and he found it hard to imagine her spilling Chinese state secrets to Westerners. Half of him thought it was more likely she had infiltrated them with a view to gathering intel and then returning to the fold. Yes, that sounded like something she might do. She had the devil in her somewhere, he knew that. Spying on new friends and flying back to the nest like a good little songbird would not be beneath the Dragonfly.

But orders were orders, and Zhou had been very clear. She was to be hunted down and killed, and all of her new friends must share the same fate. He sighed and closed his eyes. Rat would be easy to recruit. He was called Rat for a reason and wouldn't turn down the chance to kill. Pig would also not represent too many problems. Thanks to some pretty chunky mahjong gambling debts he would be grateful for the extra cash. Then there was Monkey. He wondered not only if he could find Monkey, but if it was a good idea in the first place. Monkey was highly unpredictable and difficult to manage. But he was also the very best at what he did.

"Daddy!"

He turned to see the little girl. She was growing so fast, now just a couple of months past her fifth birthday.

"Darling, how are you?"

"Fine," she said.

"And how was school today?"

"Boring."

Behind her in the kitchen he saw his wife. She was unpacking a grocery bag of vegetables but stopped to smile at him. She didn't know what he did. She thought he worked in the payroll department at the Ministry. It was better that way.

His daughter skipped back up the garden path and disappeared inside the house.

He nodded his head at some long-vanished thought and returned his attention to the songbirds as he started to plan Agent Dragonfly's assassination.

Orders were orders.

CHAPTER TWENTY-SEVEN

Paititi

Hiding deep in the jungles of Madre de Dios, seventy-five miles northeast of Machu Picchu, the vague outline of a ruined city slowly made itself visible to the team as their choppers began to descend. A casual observer might have seen nothing but a jumble of odd shapes and dismissed it as natural, like the Pyramids of Paratoari, but Hawke knew different. Among the tangled vines, orchids and rubber trees far below was the Lost City of the Incas.

"Told you I remembered," Ryan said.

"Take a look at it," Hawke said through the comms. "It's built around an extinct volcano."

"So it is," said Lexi. "At least we *hope* it's extinct." She stared down at the amazing sight of Paititi and almost couldn't believe her own eyes as she looked at the ruins and roads of the Lost City. Only in a jungle nearly twice the size of India could such a place go undiscovered for so long.

"Do volcanoes still erupt around here?" Scarlet asked.

They heard Ryan laugh over the comms. "This is Peru. Yes."

As Hawke piloted the helicopter slowly toward what he silently hoped would be their final destination, his mind was on more than the volcano. Somewhere down there, Dirk Kruger and his thugs were hard at work on their mission to loot the famous lost treasure, and the ECHO team was badly depleted and in the middle of nowhere with zero support should things go wrong. Factoring in Ziad Saqqal and his circus of biowarfare nutcases only amped things up to an even more insane degree.

He had lost too many good friends in this struggle, and the thought of failing any more members of the team weighed heavily on his mind. He flared the Bell's nose and slowed to a hover as he searched for somewhere to land among the rainforest-covered ruins.

He lowered the collective, reducing power to the engine and brought the chopper slowly down into the jungle landscape, landing in a small clearing just a few hundred meters from the eastern slopes of the volcano. In this terrifyingly vast landscape he had given up trying to see any sign of Saqqal or Kruger but suddenly a bright flash in the trees to his north startled him. He looked again and saw the sun reflecting off the South African's helicopter. Two rebels were standing around it and smoking, presumably under orders to stay and guard the chopper.

"You owe me a hundred sols, Cairo," he said smugly through the comms.

She looked at him and furrowed her brow. "How so?"

With one hand on the cyclic and the other on the collective, Hawke jutted his chin in the direction where he had seen the flash. "Over there, to the north – Kruger's parked his air-crane up."

She peered through her mirrored aviator shades before lifting them up for a second look. "Oh, bugger it. I was *certain* the stupid twat was going to get lost."

"Aren't you forgetting something" Hawke said.

"What?"

Lea spoke up over the comms from the other chopper. "She won't pay up. I'm telling ya now."

"I'm sure she will," Reaper said.

"Ah, get out of it," the Irishwoman said with a laugh. "She's tighter than a camel's arse in a sandstorm. You'll not get any silver out of her."

"I can't say this doesn't hurt," Scarlet said. "I've always paid my debts."

Then Lexi's cool voice drifted over the comms. "So where's the money?"

"Yeah, Cairo?" Hawke said. "Hand it over."

Scarlet rolled her eyes and surrendered, pulling a squashed, folded purple banknote out of her jeans pocket and pushing it inside Hawke's shirt pocket with pursed lips and a withering glance. "Happy now?"

"Funnily enough, I actually *do* feel a little better."

Before she had a chance to reply they were on the ground, and Hawke was powering down the chopper and unbuckling his seatbelt.

They climbed out of the chopper and waited while Reaper landed then Mi-171 beside the Bell and then wandered over to meet the others. Lea took a long deep breath of the mountain air as she took in the sunshine. The ruins of the city were a few hundred yards in front of them now, and looming high above it was the volcano.

"Right, let's get going," Hawke said. "It's not far to reach the volcano."

Scarlet lowered her sunglasses over her eyes from her forehead and looked up. "Shit – did I just see some smoke coming out the top of that thing?"

Hawke sighed. "No, now give it a rest."

"This is pretty amazing," Lea said, marvelling at the ruins. "Don't you think, Ry?"

Ryan said nothing.

Hawke knew what she was trying to do – pull him back into the team, back into the mission... but it was pretty obvious Ryan wasn't interested. They had all had longer to adjust to Maria's loss, but Ryan had only been hit with the news a few hours ago, and he was closest to her. The best play was to leave him alone.

Lexi stared up at the ruins ahead of them. "I can't believe we discovered the Lost City of the Incas."

"Don't get cocky," Hawke said. "Technically Dirk Kruger and his scumbags discovered it because they got here first."

"I still can't believe it," she said. "No matter who got here first."

They kept up the pace, hacking their way through the jungle with their machetes and making about as good time as anyone would in the circumstances. A tropical rainstorm skirted them to the west and for a few moments they were surrounded by a heavy, humid drizzle, but it quickly passed and they went on unhindered.

They made their way over to the ruins, scanning the area for any sign of Kruger's thugs, but with no sign of them they continued into the heart of the Lost City. As they got closer they saw there was nothing among the ruins except the broken down stones of the buildings – crumbling limestone and bromeliads crawling over granite blocks.

"I don't mean to be a spoilsport or anything," Scarlet said. "But this place isn't exactly brimming with gold and emeralds."

"No," Lexi said, also disappointed. "It's like someone got here before us."

"Maybe they did," Reaper said with a shrug of disinterest. "Enough people have looked for the place over the centuries. All the stories we heard about from explorers are just the failures, peut-être? Maybe the ones who really found it kept the treasure as well as the secret. In which case, mes amis, les carottes sont cuites, non?"

"Eh?" Hawke said.

"It is a fait accompli. There is nothing we can do about it."

Lea sighed. "At least it means that old bastard Kruger never got his hands on any of it."

"But what a waste of time, not to mention money," Scarlet said, and kicked a rock out of the way with the toe of her boot.

"We don't know anything about the place yet," Hawke said, trying to keep things together. "We keep going."

Scarlet spun her head around and drew her gun in one liquid move that took less than a second. "Did you see something move over there in the vines?"

"Like what?" Ryan said, anxious.

"I don't know. I thought I saw something move."

"It's nothing," Hawke said. "Keep going."

They passed another few hundred yards of crumbling homes and winding side streets and with each step the volcano that loomed above the houses grew larger and larger in their view.

They stopped as the hill became a steep incline. "This is the base of the volcano," Lea said.

"A tunnel!" said Lexi.

"No, it's no tunnel," Ryan said running his hand over the wall.

"You mean someone carved this?" Lea said. "Holy crap."

"No, not that either. This is a lava tube. It's a conduit created when molten lava continues flowing beneath lava that has already hardened. It's called a pāhoehoe flow, from the Hawaiian for smooth lava."

"It certainly looks more promising that those knackered old ruins behind us," Scarlet said, peering inside the tube.

"It's a tunnel that leads inside a frigging volcano," Lea said. "This is not promising."

"Tube, not tunnel," Ryan said.

Hawke pulled out the Maglite and shone it into the lava tube. As he cast the beam down to the sandy floor he grinned and nodded his head. "I see Kruger and our Syrian friends have been this way – footprints."

They made their way into the volcano, noticing an increase in the terrific humidity as soon the breeze could no longer reach them. They followed Kruger's scuff marks until they reached a steep incline in the lava tube.

After scrambling up through the tube they reached a square antechamber constructed of smooth, granite blocks. It was empty with a sand-covered floor and there was one door directly opposite them.

"Looks like the rooms in the Egyptian pyramids," Ryan said. "Definitely man-made."

"Let's keep going," Hawke said. "We can look at this on the way out."

They went through the far door and after walking along another short tunnel they emerged into sunlight again. Stretching out ahead of them around the hole leading to the magma chamber in the bottom of the volcano was something that made them all speechless.

"The Lost City!"

"Shit!"

"Buggering hell," Scarlet said. "It's made of gold."

"It really is some kind of utopia," Ryan said.

"A utopia with Saqqal and Kruger in it," Reaper said cautiously.

Scarlet started off down the slope toward the golden, vine-covered buildings. "So let's go and join the party."

CHAPTER TWENTY-EIGHT

As they walked into the city, they were mesmerized by the stunning metropolis stretching away from them in every direction. It was a wonderful, terrible ghost town and they walked in silence for a long time. The sunlight shone in through the vent in the top of the volcano and sparkled and glittered on the golden, jewel-encrusted walls. It held Lea like a hypnotist's watch, and she couldn't lift her eyes away no matter how hard she tried. She didn't even want to.

"In all my years of doing this," she said quietly. "I have never, *ever* seen anything like this place."

"I want to marry it," Scarlet said.

"Don't be ridiculous," Reaper said.

"Why is that ridiculous?" she replied, transfixed by the immeasurable beauty and wealth before her. "I read about someone who married his car once, and I want to marry this city."

"But imagine the prenup," Lexi said with a sideways glance.

Slowly they made their way through the old streets as they twisted and meandered their way deeper into the abandoned city. Ancient ruins loomed either side of them, their crumbling architecture a sad testament to their incredible age.

"It's actually quite eerie," Lexi said, tracing her finger along a wall as she walked. "I mean, there are so many old houses here, and rooms... I think I can feel eyes on me all the time."

"You think someone's watching us?" Reaper said.

"Not exactly… I'm just creeped out by this place, that's all."

"The architecture is amazing," Lea said. "Don't you think, Ry?"

"If you say so."

"Just a shame Luis never made it," she said quietly. "Or Professor Balta."

"Damn right," Hawke said. "Kruger can pay for that along with everything else as soon as we catch up with him. Maria, Luis, Balta… the way he treated Ryan. He's going to pay for it all."

Further in the city, the atmosphere started to change. Somewhere high up above their heads they heard the cry of a king vulture. Looking up, Lexi watched the startled bird leap from a ledge and fly up into the throat of the volcano. It heaved its body into the crater on massive black wings and vanished over the rim.

"Not digging this, Joe," Lea said.

They turned from the vulture and looked at Lea. "What is it?"

She pointed to what looked like some kind of temple. "Look on the wall – recognize it?"

Hawke recognized it all right. Scratched into the wall above the shrine were two Greek letters: ΑΘ. "Bugger."

"My sentiments exactly. How the hell is the sign of the Athanatoi carved into a wall on the inside of a lava cave in deepest, darkest Peru?"

"Simple explanation," Reaper said. "We're not the first to find this place. The Immortals already got here."

"And check this out," Scarlet said, further along the cave wall. "Another set of the Greek letters inside a weird, standing man, and all around him are people on their knees."

"They're worshipping him!"

"Worshipping the Athanatoi?"

Their awed silence was broken by the sound of a gunshot and then screaming. The yelling was Kruger, as usual, and he was barking commands once again.

"Where did it come from?" Ryan asked,

"Sodding echo makes it hard to tell," Lea said.

Reaper turned three-sixty as he looked down all the streets leading away from the temple area. "I think over there, to the north."

They pushed on, still lit from above but the sun's illumination was growing weaker. What was bright Peruvian sunshine was now a thin, watery light thanks to the many filters of vines it had to pass through before it reached them far below on the floor of the volcano.

Hawke thought once again about the people who had been following them... He hadn't told the others because he didn't want to freak them out, but that time was fast running out. He knew who they were, or at least he knew who he *thought* they were. They'd been trailing them since they climbed out of the chopper, and yet had stayed almost completely out of sight. If it hadn't been for his extensive training in jungle warfare he would never had known they were there, on their tail.

He knew they were from some kind of Amazonian tribe. That was obvious, but what intrigued Hawke was the idea that they were simply guarding their home, and that this place was their territory... that Paititi, the Lost City of the Incas, known to the entire world for centuries in countless legends and myths, was simply someone's home. If that was the truth, then he strongly doubted they'd ever had contact with any other humans, and that could make them either easier to handle, or extremely unpredictable and dangerous. Worse than that, there was no way to know how many of them there were and they had the home advantage. To say it was not an ideal situation was a wild understatement.

Lea sighed. "Where is that bastard Kruger?"

"There!" Scarlet said. "They're down there."

"Speak of Cao Cao and Cao Cao arrives,' Lexi said.

Using the northern city wall for cover they looked down toward the northern edge of the volcano and saw Saqqal and Kruger and the others. The men were standing well back from the bank of a very small river in front of a strange shrine, and all were wearing NBC suits. The shrine was ornate enough at the base, but the top was what freaked them all out – a humanoid figure with two long, twisted horns protruding from its head, a devilish fanged grin on its face and two wild, crazed eyes staring back at the city.

"Okay, two questions," Lea said. "Why are they wearing those suits, and what the hell is that thing with the horns?"

"Supay," Ryan said. "The Incan god of death. As for the suits, I can't help you."

"Oh, *excellent*," Lea said. "I never said anything to you guys but I was *so* hoping we'd end up fighting another god of death."

Hawke frowned. "The suits worry me more."

Saqqal ordered Rajavi to get something out of a large bag and moments later he produced a shining steel container not much bigger than a lunch box. Jawad pointed and said a few words, and in response Kruger and Corzo took a few more steps back from the water.

"What are they *doing?*" Lexi asked.

Hawke watched the men. "Something tells me they're not here for the gold and diamonds."

Scarlet brushed some hair away from her eyes. "Those suits are not a good development in this mission."

Lea heard nothing, but she felt it.

A sharp, stabbing pain between her shoulder blades.

She turned and gasped when she saw the Indian tribesmen behind them.

Hawke turned but it was too late. At least a dozen warriors were standing around them, all armed with spears and arrows and blowpipes. Their silent footfall had allowed them to creep up within feet of them.

A man with a strange criss-cross tattoo on his face waved his spear in Hawke's face and indicated he should get up and raise his hands in the air.

Hawke followed the instructions and the others followed suit, and then the tattooed man called out in a strange language and Dirk Kruger looked up. His face was obscured behind the gas mask and hard to see, but Hawke guessed he wasn't smiling.

The South African archaeologist shouted back a string of commands in the tribesman's language and the next thing he knew they were being marched down to the river bank with their hands above their heads.

CHAPTER TWENTY-NINE

The Syrian general had stopped them at least a hundred yards from the river, more out of concern for the tribe than the ECHO team, and now Hawke stared at Kruger and felt his blood rising. He had faced many enemies in his life, but never had he experienced anything like he was feeling now. The man he was staring at, this *bastard*, had put Ryan Bale through hell and threatened his young life. Now, he was threatening the lives of the few good friends he had left after the carnage of the Seastead battle.

"What's the matter, Englishman?" Kruger crowed. "Not used to losing?"

Hawke said nothing.

"The fucking cat got your tongue, or what?" Kruger said. As he spoke, Rajavi padded over to them with a gun in his hands.

Scarlet took a step forward and sneered. "Is that gas mask how Mrs Kruger likes it in bed?"

Kruger gave the order and Rajavi slapped Scarlet into the dirt, and then all the men in gas masks laughed for a few moments. Kruger walked over to them and took a deep breath as he surveyed the gigantic volcano cave. "Think about how many stupid bastards tried to find this place!" he said, and then he raised his voice to a maniacal shout. "And now it's all mine!"

When his voice had finished echoing off the cave walls, Lea spoke up. "It's only fitting considering that you're the biggest stupid bastard of them all."

Kruger reached out and grabbed her by the hair, pulling her head down to waist height and starting to shake it around as he yelled in her face. "Maybe you should be a little nicer to this stupid bastard before he blows your fucking head off?"

Hawke lunged forward, never wanting to kill a man more than this, but before he got five yards Rajavi stepped in and beat him to the ground with his rifle stock.

Kruger smirked. "Now be nice and quiet while we get on with our business."

Saqqal sent Rajavi and Corzo to the shore of the underground river. Despite their NBC suits, neither looked very happy about going, but they obeyed, and moments later they collected a sample of damp soil from the riverbed.

Saqqal then ordered Dr Jawad forward with his soil-testing kit. The bacteriologist padded forward through the rubble and moss, stumbling occasionally on pieces of loose rock before finally reaching the sample.

"It's never a nice feeling," Scarlet said, "when you're the only one in a room full of people wearing NBC suits."

"What sort of parties do you go to?" Lexi said.

Over the next few minutes Bashir Jawad worked diligently on the riverbank while Rajavi kept the ECHO team in place with his submachine gun. With the silicon face under the NBC suit he was the man behind the mask behind the mask, and it looked even weirder than usual.

Hawke stepped back, keeping one eye on the bacteriologist and the other firmly fixed on Rajavi who was still holding the submachine gun in his face.

Saqqal took a couple of steps forward, a look of anxious expectancy in the eyes lurking behind the NBC face mask. The humidity in the small cavern was high, and they were all covered in a persistent film of sweat.

"Well?" Saqqal snapped.

Jawad turned and looked faintly ridiculous as he nodded in the NBC suit.

Saqqal gasped audibly and turned to Kruger, shaking his hand. "Then that confirms it. Well done, Mr Kruger! You have been true to your word. I will wire one hundred million dollars into your account as soon as we're in Rio and the rest of this city is yours to gut at any time you choose."

"What the hell is this?" Hawke said.

Kruger turned to him. "Meet *Utopia*... a bacterial infection totally unknown to modern science. Think of it as a sort of mutated halfway house between the bubonic plague and anthrax, capable of existing outside of both reservoir and vector for an almost limitless time. Its power is in its will to live... the fastest bacteria we know doubles every four hours, but not this stuff. In the hour we've been here our tests show it doubles every few minutes – but only when exposed to the atmosphere. When it's underwater it reproduces at a normal rate. But if this is released into the air outside it will mutate and reproduce while airborne into a devastating cloud of death."

"And you're waking it from the dead to play with it," Lea said in disgust. "You are absolutely out of your freaking mind."

"That is distinctly possible," Kruger said with a dismissive glance emanating from behind the mask. "My friend the general here is of the opinion it can also be weaponized. The deal is I get all the lost treasure for myself and another one hundred million on top, and he gets the nasties in the river."

"You're going to allow him to spread this thing across the world?"

"Not the world – just the United States and Europe, and of course – only after we have created an antidote for ourselves."

"But why?" Lea said.

Saqqal replied, his voice cold and hard. "It is time for the pestilent West to be annihilated and wiped from the surface of this world. Only then may we grow spiritually as a people and know real peace." He paused and indicated the vast city of gold behind them "Do you think the people of a city like this would just give it up? Why do you think the Incas disappeared from history so fast? The answer, my friends, is Utopia. It wiped them all out, and that is what I intend to do to the West! Only then will the world be liberated." He held the vial up to the light streaming down from the crater and stared at it through the goggles in his gas mask.

"If you had a mind you've be out of it," Hawke said.

"Your pathetic insults mean nothing to me," Saqqal said. "Besides, there's already a good chance you've already contracted Utopia. It has been dormant beneath the water for countless centuries, and drinking the water would be fatal, naturally. Whether or not you have caught it we cannot tell, but you should know that Dr Jawad here considers it to be highly contagious... as history has shown."

"And what about the tribe?" Lea said. "Don't you care about them?"

"No," Saqqal said flatly.

Hawke shook his head in disgust. "If I were you I'd scare myself. You're a madman!"

Saqqal gave a shallow nod of evaluation as if he were seriously weighing the possibility in his mind. "Perhaps."

"Isn't this treasure enough for you?" Lea said, taking another step back from the river.

"And what can treasure give me that Utopia cannot? With the power to realign global politics and wipe out as much of the human population wherever I choose I will have something much greater than a pile of gold plates and jewel-encrusted statues. Your problem is that you do not think big enough."

"My problem right now is that you're insane."

"If I am insane then I have been drive mad by the lust for revenge. Three years ago the American fighters killed my family while they slept in their beds. The rage grew inside me until it was no longer containable. I have had much time to consider what it's like to feel that much anger coursing through your veins night and day. I wonder if it has driven me to a kind of madness." He turned to face Hawke. "But the thing is I don't care at all. All I care about is that the people who murdered my wife and children will now pay a truly unthinkable price, and they will pay that price to me – Ziad Saqqal."

Lea had been edging closer to Rajavi, and suddenly she made a lunge for the submachine gun. She grappled with him for the gun and almost got her hands on the handle but then the Iranian saw what she was doing and swiftly pulled it away.

Hawke burst into action but Kruger whipped a pistol out of his belt and told him to get back.

Now, Rajavi was moving his hands up around Lea's neck and beginning to choke her. Up close she was even more terrified by the weird mask and struggled to get out of his grip. His breathing became more rapid under the silicon layer and the only sign of humanity was his crazed, bloodshot eyes as they blinked madly from behind the two crude slits that lurked under the NBC goggles.

She brought her knee up into his balls and he flinched but didn't let go, so she did it again and then a third time. He took one of his hands off her throat and tried to use it to stop her knee from coming up a fourth time but she was too fast and delivered the heftiest smack of them all. It did the trick and then a strange howl emanated from behind the mouth slit in the mask and he staggered back in pain.

"Enough!" Saqqal barked.

Corzo walked over and pushed Lea back to the others, and helped Rajavi to his feet. The Iranian knocked him back and snatched up the gun.

"How did you know this was here, Saqqal?" Ryan asked.

"Mr Kruger here has been studying Inca quipus for a very long time."

"Indeed, I have. You see, they are a form of semasiography, and on top of being used for purposes of arithmetic they were also used for recording other narratives, such as myths, legends and much more prosaic things like diaries. It didn't take me long to realize that the many references to a flood could be instead referring to a kind of devastating plague. And that's when the penny dropped, as you say." He turned to Ryan. "Should have stuck with me, kid."

"Drop dead," Ryan said.

Kruger turned to leave. "Sadly, it is now time to leave you in the charming company of the Paititi Tribe. I gave them that name because they were only discovered by me a few hours ago. Luckily they seem to speak a dialect of Takana or I would probably be in as much trouble as you are all in right now. As you saw, they are already smitten with me." He gave a cruel laugh and shouted at the warriors.

They leaped into action, pulling their blowpipes out and loading them up.

"What the hell's going on?" Lexi screamed.

"They're poison darts," Hawke yelled. "Look up there on the ridge about a third of the way up the volcano wall behind the shrine."

"Shit, they really *are* blowguns!" Scarlet said.

"Oh for *fuck's* sake!" Lea said. "Not more bloody blowguns and poison darts. Did we not get enough of those in friggin' Mexico?"

"Why don't you go and complain about it to them," Scarlet said. We know they've had zero contact with Western civilization so I'm sure it will all go very well. Do you know the sign language for 'please make it quick because I don't like pain'?"

"Oh, piss off, Cairo!"

Hawke's mind raced. He'd heard rumors about lost Indian tribes in the Amazon when he was training in Belize, and they weren't all that reassuring. Many people had claimed to have discovered the last lost tribe – the Mashco Piro tribe being the most recent, but like many, Hawke had his suspicions that there were plenty more out there who wished to stay lost. The Amazon rainforest was a mostly uninhabited jungle half the size of Europe so the prospect of it concealing other lost tribes wasn't exactly mind-blowing, and now they had the proof.

And it was with that thought that he turned to watch even more warriors now gathering on the upper level. They were wearing some kind of reddish clay-colored paint and held a variety of weapons besides the blowpipes.

Kruger beamed. "My new friends are going to ensure you stay where you are while we load up the choppers with the finest pieces of this wonderful treasure, and then when they see their new gods fly away, they are ordered to kill you. They tell me it is their tradition to cannibalize their dead, so you will end your days as lunch for these fine warriors."

They watched Saqqal and Kruger, still in NBC suits and flanked by Jawad, Rajavi and Corzo, as they ambled up the hill into the northern part of the city. They filled their bags with various pieces Kruger selected from the heaps of gold and gems scattered all over the city, and then they began to shuffle toward the lava tube in the southern part of the city.

Kruger called out a command which echoed through the dormant volcano and the warriors raised their blowpipes to their mouths. A second command from Kruger and they began firing the poison darts at the ECHO team.

"Run for it!" Hawke yelled.

"You think?" Scarlet said.

They clambered up the bank and dived over the wall they had used for cover but the darts kept on coming, clattering all around them as they sprinted through the deserted streets of gold.

They saw the antechamber they had used as an entrance to the Lost City as it slowly came into view and pounded their way toward it with the darts flying all around their heads and bouncing off the dirt near their boots.

"Faster!" Hawke yelled.

They finally reached the antechamber at the entrance to the lava tunnel and charged inside only to find the opposite door was shut firm.

"Bastard wedged it shut somehow," Scarlet said.

"Go back?" Ryan said.

"Er... poison darts?" Lea said.

"Oh yeah."

Reaper pulled on the handle but instead of it opening the door they had used to enter the room on their way in, the door behind them slammed shut and now they were trapped. "A booby-trap," he said, looking unusually rattled.

"All right," Hawke said. "At least we're away from those sodding darts for a second. That gives us time to think."

Above their heads they heard a grinding sound and looked up to see some kind of rigging slowly descending toward them.

Lea looked at Hawke and sighed. "You had to say it, didn't you?"

And then Lexi interrupted them. "Guys... Are there spikes on that thing?"

CHAPTER THIRTY

Hawke looked up and saw she was right. The rigging that was slowly making its way toward them was some kind of bronze framework with at least two dozen razor-sharp spikes on it. Long vines hung down like tentacles and made it look even grimmer. "This is not good," he said.

Lea searched the antechamber for anything that might indicate a way out as the rigging above their heads slowly worked its way toward them. The grinding sound of the grille as it scraped against the cooled lava was ear-piercing, and with every second the sharpened bronze spikes grew ever-closer to their heads. "Maybe we can use the vines to escape?" she said.

The liana vines covering the spike-frame were now low enough to be dangling over them. The liana was a type of woody vine that thrived in the canopies of the Amazon rainforest and some could grow over three thousand feet long. These ones had grown in through cracks in the roof the chamber.

"Possible," Ryan said glumly. "It's where they get rattan for rope and stuff."

"Well it's gross," Lea said, pulling some away from her shoulder.

"Don't worry about it," Hawke said, helping to pull the liana away from her.

Another vine slid over her back and she screamed.

"Just calm down," Hawke said.

"I *am* being calm, Josiah…"

"If this is your idea of calm I'd hate to see how you react when something serious happens, like burning the toast."

"Stop being a smartarse and just get the thing off me. It's... *gross*."

"Hey!" Ryan said. "I think I found something – look."

They joined him by the door they had used on their way into the volcano. He was studying a stone panel in the floor, positioned like a doormat and covered in strange lines.

"What is it, mate?"

"Some kind of Inca puzzle, I think. I'm not sure." He got down on his knees and blew the dust and dirt out of the cracks in the puzzle stone.

"Time to get sure, Ry," Lea said casting a panicked glare upwards. "Can't be more than a couple of minutes till that thing's turning us all into kebabs."

"I'm going as fast as I can," he said. "These are not easy to read. They're very badly deteriorated for one thing, and the meanings seem to be obscured... almost cryptic."

"That's great, Ryan," Lexi said, joining Lea now and staring up at the descending framework of razor-sharp spikes. "But in about ninety seconds we're going to be pinned to the dirt like butterflies on a piece of card."

"I believe," Ryan said, turning to face her. "That the term you're searching for is *mounting board*."

"Yes, I believe it may be," Lexi said. "Oh and by the way – why are you looking at me and not the symbols?"

"She has a point, mate."

Ryan conceded the matter and returned to the symbols. "I've been looking at these all wrong. This isn't a series of degraded symbols at all – this is a depiction of a yupana."

"And that's what?"

"It's basically an Incan abacus."

"Oh, *crap*," Scarlet said. "A maths problem."

Ryan turned to her, his face more weary now, but the faintest glimmer of the man he used to be still in his eyes. "Thank God *I'm* here then, eh?"

"Yes," she said, crossing her arms. "Quite."

"So let me get on with it, then."

Lea felt the frustration grow in her heart. They had already lost Professor Balta and Luis, and now things were looking perilous for the rest of the team as well. Not only that, but Ziad Saqqal, Jawad, Rajavi, Corzo and Dirk Kruger were all getting away with the Lost Treasure of the Incas piled into their choppers. If that weren't bad enough, they also had of the most lethal forms of pneumatic plague ever to strike mankind.

Reaper stared up at the grid, shook his head and let out a long, low sigh. It was low enough for him to reach now, and he grabbed hold of one of the spikes to test its strength. "Definitely bronze," he said, trying hard to shift it. "And connected very strongly to the grille framework. We're not snapping these things off."

"More good news," Scarlet said.

The grinding sound was louder now as the framework was working its way much closer, and they were all crouching to avoid the spikes pushing down onto their heads and shoulders.

"I've got it," Ryan said. "It's actually a rather complex mathematics puzzle – much more complex that I would have thought them capable of."

"Ryan… four inches…"

"He knows all about four inches," Scarlet said, nudging the young man in the ribs. "Eh, *boy?*"

Ryan ignored it. "It's similar to Ribet's Theorem."

Lea stared at him. "*What* now?"

"Three inches…"

"It's a number theory statement to do with the properties of Galois representations that are associated with modular forms."

Lexi looked at him. "Ryan, are you having a breakdown?"

"When the epsilon conjecture was finally proven it led the way to Fermat's Last Theorem being cracked."

Hawke scratched his head and looked from the spikes to Ryan's young face. "Mate, when you said it was a maths problem I thought you meant like adding up."

"Yeah… not so much."

"Two inches."

"Ryan definitely knows about all about *two* inches," Scarlet said.

Lea sighed. "It didn't work and wasn't funny at four inches, so why the hell do you think it would work and be funny two inches later?"

"Give me a break, I'm under pressure!"

On their knees now, the spikes were only inches away from them, and there was nowhere else to run or hide. "Can't be more than thirty seconds before we're all skewered," Lexi said. "Not how I thought I was going to go out."

"And how did you think you were going to go out?" Hawke asked.

She shrugged. I don't know… maybe in battle, or in the basement of the Ministry under heavy interrogation. What about you?"

"Me?" Hawke said. "Not the sort of thing I think about."

"And you?" Lexi asked Scarlet.

"Oh, no idea. Maybe massaged to death on a tropical beach with a banana daiquiri in each hand."

Lea rolled her eyes. "Yes, how very *you*."

"Thanks, darling."

"It wasn't a compliment, and ouch! Blood hell, Ryan – hurry up! These sodding spikes are starting to push into my shoulders!"

"I'm going as fast as I can, Lea."

"So how about you?" Lexi asked Lea.

"Me? I don't know. Not as a freaking kebab to be discovered in another two hundred years by another idiot searching for gold plates, that's for damned sure!"

With seconds to spare, Ryan arranged the tiles and the frame stopped descending. A few seconds later the door opened, but the one behind, blocking the Amazonian warriors, stayed shut.

"Thanks buggery for that," Scarlet said, rubbing her shoulder. "It was getting rather poky in there."

"Oh, *please...*" Lea said.

They raced through the lava tunnel and emerged in the outside of the volcano into the fresh air. They ran through the jumble of stone houses in the outer quarter until they got back to the clearing beyond the town.

Just as they had predicted, there was no sign of Kruger, Saqqal or the chopper outside the volcano. They had cleared out with all of the treasure and the dead bodies of both the rebels were lying around the area where they had taken off.

"Why did he kill his own men?" Ryan asked.

"To make room for the treasure," Hawke said with disgust, and then sighed as he turned his face toward the trees to the south where he had landed. Smoke was billowing up into the tropical sky. "Looks like they blew up our choppers as well."

They all turned to face the scene of destruction in the distant jungle and walked slowly along the path they had hiked on their way to the volcano just hours ago. When they reached the clearing they saw Hawke had been

187

right in his guess – both the Bell 47 and the Mi-171 were now just smouldering wreckage, courtesy of Rajavi's grenade launcher.

Hawke clenched his jaw with anger as he thought about Kruger and Saqqal laughing as their helicopters exploded, while they were fighting for their lives back in the spike trap. "These bastards are really beginning to get on my nerves," he said through gritted teeth.

"We'll get him, don't worry about that," Scarlet said coolly. "I always get my man."

"And everyone else's," Lexi said with a sideways glance.

"Oh, that's rich coming from you," Scarlet said, fronting up to her.

"And what is *that* supposed to mean?"

"Pack it in," Hawke said.

"So what now?" Lea asked.

"Now we wait for Lund to send back up," Reaper said.

Hawke nodded. "Thank God we told him the coordinates…"

Lea turned to him. "You think we can trust him?"

He shrugged he shoulders. "I hope so, because if we can't, it's a twenty day hike in that direction." He pointed through a cloud of mosquitoes at the jungle beyond the clearing.

CHAPTER THIRTY-ONE

It turned out they could trust Lund, and when they failed to check in with their report from Paititi, he arranged for the Peruvian authorities to send rescue choppers out to get them. They also sent a team of archaeologists from the National Museum of Archaeology, Anthropology and History based in Lima.

After a brief handover the ECHO team were airborne once again and flying back to Cusco where their jet was fuelled and waiting for them. Lund had run the situation through what he called his 'washing machine' but come up with very little information about Kruger's whereabouts. It seemed his arms didn't have quite the same reach as those of Sir Richard Eden. From Saqqal's bragging back in the volcano they knew they were returning to Rio de Janeiro, but they needed more than that so their only chance was Alex Reeve and her CIA contacts.

Hawke called her on his cell phone but there was no answer, so he left a voicemail message and settled back into his seat while he waited for a reply. He failed in his attempt to suppress a yawn and then pushed back in the soft leather seat of the private jet. According to the little screen on the partition wall, they were climbing out of twenty-thousand feet and somewhere above the Peruvian-Bolivian border. Their bearing was sixty-seven degrees and the ETA was in just under three and a half hours.

Reaper was once again crashed on the leather couch on the jet's portside, and Lexi, Scarlet and Ryan were playing poker at the table in the rear of the aircraft. It was fairly subdued, but then they got on the subject of SUVs and when Ryan told Scarlet that Pajero meant wanker in Spanish she burst into uncontrollable laughter for what seemed a lot longer than it probably was.

Lea had brought a coffee and sat beside him, but the coffee was in the little cup-holder, untouched and now she was dozing in her seat. For a moment he watched her, wondering how she had turned out so right when everything had been so against her, and then his phone rang.

"It's me, Joe."

"It's good to hear your voice, Alex," he said.

"Yours too," she replied.

"How's life in Fort Belvoir Community Hospital?"

"Sucks."

"Thought it might."

A long pause.

"Dad just left a few minutes ago."

"And how many people get visited in hospital by the President of the United States?"

"President-*elect*, if you don't mind. He's not the Commander-in-Chief until he's sworn in on Inauguration Day."

"I think it's a bit late for denial, Agent Nightingale."

"You may have a point," she said, and he heard a gentle, sad laugh. "And on that..."

He waited but there were no words. "What is it?"

"Dad wants me to stay here in DC now. It's confirmed."

"And what do you think?"

"I don't know. There were some pretty serious-looking faces behind him when he asked me."

Hawke nodded gently in the dim light of the Gulfstream, even though she was over three thousand miles away and couldn't see him. To his right, a sleeping Lea turned on her side and rested her head on his shoulder.

"So am I going to get a tour of the White House or not?" he said. He knew by her tone she had already made up her mind about DC.

"Sure. Well, everyone except Scarlet. No way is she getting through vetting."

He laughed, and almost woke Lea. "You might have a point there. She's not exactly Oval Office material. She spent half of today chewing coca leaves."

"Huh?"

"Long story – listen do you have the information I need?"

"Sure – according to the port authority there's a Navetta moored in the Rio docks and it's registered to Kruger Mining Corps. It's been in the port for over a week so I'm guessing he had his men sail it from Cape Town to Rio in advance with a view to bringing the treasure home after he'd discovered it."

"He's a cocky little bastard then, isn't he?"

"So it would appear."

"And what about Saqqal?"

"Apart form his Hezbollah stuff there's nothing on him that could help us here at all. They're travelling together, if that's any use, but other than that I got nothing."

"Great."

"But Dad greased some wheels in the US Embassy in Brasilia so I think the Brazilians are sorting some back-up for you."

"All right – thanks, Alex. I don't know what I'd do without you."

She paused before replying. "Sure."

"What?"

"Nothing."

"Nothing?"

"All right… Joe, listen…"

He was interrupted by Lea. "I have to go, Alex."

He cut the call as Lea approached. She had her phone in her hand too and was ending a call. "That was the American ambassador in Brasília. Alex worked her magic with her father I guess because he just told me he's spoken with the Minister of Justice and they've sanctioned the use of a BOPE squad in response to the threat posed by Saqqal."

"BOPE?" Lexi asked.

"Batalhão de Operações Policiais Especias," Scarlet replied without hesitation. She looked at them. "What?"

"You speak Portuguese?" Hawke asked.

"Oh, God no," she replied. "Only a couple of phrases."

"I bet," Lea said. "Don't tell me – *are there many sailors here?* and *I've never seen this gun before in all my life.*"

"I'm going to ignore that slur," she replied coolly. "BOPE are a counter-terrorism force, sort of a Brazilian SWAT. They'll be less use than an SAS squad but more use than an SBS one."

"Piss off."

"With pleasure."

"They're meeting us at the docks, anyway," Lea said.

"What about Alex?"

"She's staying in DC for the foreseeable future," Hawke said with a sigh.

"Lazy cow's just trying to get out of rebuilding Elysium," Scarlet said.

*

Ziad Saqqal pushed back into the jet's leather seat and closed his eyes as his mind raked over the last few hours of his life. The lethal monster currently squirming around in Jawad's carry case would bring devastation to the United States and any other country he desired, but first he knew he had to test it – and before he crossed the ocean and went to Africa. He had the perfect place in mind.

"Just make sure it's nowhere near me," Kruger said with a grim look at the case.

Saqqal agreed it would be a bad thing to anywhere near it when it was released. Jawad had patiently explained with the quiet blandness of the expert that sixty percent of Londoners were killed by the Black Death in the six months from the autumn of 1348 into the start of 1349. It was total devastation, and without a single sword unsheathed the population of whole nations was decimated. Thanks to old research, most people believed the plague was transmitted from person to person by filthy fleas or rats, when the truth was far darker.

New research of the disease's vector from the British military science facility at Porton Down in England was pointing to something extremely grim... the plague was passed from person to person by airborne transmission. Yes... a simple sneeze or cough would be enough to pass the plague from you to the next man or woman and so two infected people became four, and four became eight. He smiled at the thought of the Utopia bacteria dividing to grow stronger, and how they used people in the same way, like marionettes to further their own agenda.

Millions of people dying a slow, agonizing death from shock and respiratory failure would be more than enough revenge for him, and the people of Rio de

Janeiro would be the first to sample the delights locked away in Dr Jawad's sweaty grasp. The NBC suits were all they needed to ensure their survival when the horror unfolded, and then they would flee the country on Kruger's boat.

"Just make sure your boat is ready," Saqqal said. "Something tells me Rio de Janeiro isn't going to be a very pleasant place for the next few years."

CHAPTER THIRTY-TWO

Rio de Janeiro

Scarlet Sloane knew she had it in her heart to care when she saw the sun setting over Guanabara Bay on the final approach to Rio. She had been here before, but not for many years, and it wasn't business either. Instead, she had met with an old lover and spent some time reliving the old days. It was a turbocharged week fuelled by cachaça and Derby cigarettes. They'd got wasted and lost a lot of money gambling illegally on jogo de bucho, but it was a week to remember. She smiled at the memory because times like those were the only thing that kept her sane.

Now, their jet descended over the bay and landed on the small island of Galeão where the city's main international airport was located. She watched without emotion as the plane trundled to the apron and the pilot activated the airstair. Moments later the humid Brazilian air was flooding into the air-conditioned cabin and she was in yet another country but with no time to enjoy it.

Kruger had barely more than an hour's lead on them but his plane was slower and they had almost caught up with him. With luck he would still be at the airport, and the same went for the Syrian madmen with the Utopia bioweapon. She looked outside and saw the day was nearly over. The twilight in Rio vanished fast, but that would be to their advantage. If Kruger was occupied loading the Lost Treasure onto a truck to take to his boat he would be distracted enough, but whatever guard he'd

195

set up would be easier to approach and attack under cover of night.

Customs seemed to take longer than usual, a chore Scarlet Sloane was rarely able to tolerate with anything resembling good grace, but at least it was taking place on board their private jet and not in the airport.

They left the aircraft and began searching for Saqqal's plane on the aprons provided for private aircraft. They walked up and down on the hot asphalt searching for the aircraft when suddenly they found them. Rajavi and Corzo were loading the gold into an SUV while Saqqal, Kruger and Jawad were talking to an airport official. Kruger handed the young man a large envelope which Hawke presumed was a bribe.

A man in a dark suit approached the ECHO team and introduced himself as Sergeant Carvalho of the Military Police of Rio de Janeiro. He was a solid man with a chunky handshake and dark, honest eyes.

"We're watching them just as we were instructed," Carvalho said with a subtle nod across the tarmac at the SUV.

It was then that Kruger saw them, and they scattered. Kruger and Corzo dived into the SUV and skidded off the apron while Saqqal, Jawad and Rajavi piled into a catering truck and made off in the opposite direction.

"Wait – Saqqal's making a break for it!"

"Eh?"

"He's not going with Kruger to the boat – he's got another plan!"

"Great," Scarlet said. "The sodding BOPE team are down at the docks."

"Fine," Hawke said. "You get down there and stop Kruger leaving the country with the treasure. Lea and I will take Saqqal down. There's only three of them."

Reaper, Lexi, Scarlet and Ryan followed Carvalho to his car.

"And what about us now?" Lea said. "Saqqal's getting away and we haven't even got a flaming car!"

A pushback tug trundled past them on its way to a 737 landing on the nearest runway.

"By Strength and Guile, Donovan... and we mean it!"

Hawke ran alongside the tug, pulled the man out and revved the engine. He had no idea how fast these things went but he was about to find out. He floored the throttle as he weaved the tug in and out of a baggage train, and soon discovered the answer to his question – twenty-five miles per hour.

From the noise the engine was making it already sounded like it was pretty unhappy at the treatment he was giving it, so he frantically searched the airfield for an alternative as he pursued Saqqal. Ahead, his prayers were answered by three bright red fire trucks in front of the airport fire station, and he raced the pushback tractor as fast as it would go across the grass, wildly cutting over a runway just as a Boeing 747 was about to land, forcing it to go around. He guessed he wasn't too popular either on board the aircraft or in the Air Traffic Control tower but there was no time worry about it. He could live with being deported from Brazil if it meant stopping whatever lunacy Ziad Saqqal had in store.

He pulled the pushback tug up to one of the fire trucks and climbed inside. The keys were in the ignition, saving him the effort and time of hotwiring it, and seconds later he and Lea were skidding off the apron in pursuit of the catering truck which was almost at the exit to the airport.

Hawke swung the truck around to the right and noticed in his mirror that the truck's boom-ladder was loose and now swinging wildly from left to right as he swerved in his pursuit of the Syrians. Clearly the training that the firemen were doing back at the station hadn't finished yet, and he was just going to have to live with it.

"He's almost out of the airport!" Lea said.

"I'm going as fast as I can!" said Hawke.

"Why don't you put the siren and lights on?" she asked as she loaded her gun. "That makes it go faster."

"Of course it doesn't bloody well make it go..." he looked at her and saw the look she was giving him. "Ah, right."

"You're such a dope, Joe Hawke."

She leaned out of the window of the cab and fired a couple of shots at the catering truck, but they missed. They were too far away for any meaningful shot with a handgun, but at least she gave it a shot, he thought. He spun the wheel hard to the left and slammed his boot down on the throttle, sending the truck skidding hard in a sharp arc and the boom flying off to their right.

"What the hell are you doing, ya eejit?"

He pointed over to the other side of the airfield. "They're going over there. We can cut them off."

"Sure we can, except for the fact there's a bloody great razorwire fence all the way around the sodding airfield."

"Oh yeah – I didn't see that," he said giving her a sideways glance and rolling his eyes. "However will we get through a chain-link fence with nothing but a ten ton fire truck at our disposal?"

"Smartarse, that's what ya are. A right little smartarse... but with nice eyes."

The offending fence was now coming up fast as the truck raced toward the airport's perimeter. "Cover your eyes!" he yelled.

Lea looked away and Hawke lowered his head as the fire truck smashed through the fence at speed, snagging a panel of it in the front fender and dragging it along behind them as they launched off the kerb and slammed down on the road running around the airfield.

"Christ almighty that was idiotic!" she said. "But also kinda fun."

"I'm glad you approve."

When he had stabilized the truck, he powered it forward once again, keeping a close eye on the catering truck as it tried to outrun them on the ring road. He felt a heavy clunking sound and checked his mirror to see the boom-ladder had become partially unfixed to the top of the truck and was now hanging limply behind them, scraping along the asphalt in a shower of orange sparks.

"You're never driving my car, I can tell ya that."

"They let you drive?"

He stamped on the brakes and the heavy truck juddered violently as he brought the speed down low enough to take the corner, but they were making progress. Up ahead the old catering truck had run into the heavier traffic of the Sâo Cristóvâo district and Saqqal was having to work harder to make his escape, but Hawke still had no idea where that was. He would have thought they wanted to get on a plane as fast as possible, but they were driving away from the airport instead. He guessed they had access to a private airfield but he was damned sure they weren't going to get there.

They chased the catering truck south through the suburb of Rio Comprido before Saqqal took a sharp right at Cosme Velho and raced into the mountains to the north of Copacabana. Now they were racing along a boulevard lined with jacaranda trees and expensive sedans.

"Not a private airfield then…" Hawke said.

Lea watched suburbia fly past them. "Where the hell is he going?"

Then Hawke pointed to a large mass of land rising up ahead of them to the southeast. "My best guess is he's going to have a chat with God."

She looked at him, confused "Eh?"

"Up there," he said, and pointed to the sky. "See what I mean?"

She stared up at the twilight where a grove of sparkling stars studded the sky like diamonds and her eyes widened with amazement. "Oh… *wow!*"

CHAPTER THIRTY-THREE

Vincent Reno and the others followed Carvalho through a utility corridor until they reached a door which opened out to a small car park. Carvalho blipped the locks on a Chevy Blazer and seconds later they were skidding out of the airport and driving down to the docks.

"My men are already in place," the Brazilian said. "There is no way for the South Africans to leave the city with the stolen treasure."

Scarlet leaned over into the front. "Is the air conditioning on, or what?"

"Broken," Carvalho said with regret. "Only the heater works."

"Oh, that's okay then," the Englishwoman said. "It's only thirty-nine degrees with ninety percent humidity today – why not turn the heater on instead?"

Carvalho smiled and offered a polite laugh, but made no reply. He used his knowledge of the city to weave the Blazer neatly in and out of the Rio traffic, passing south through the districts of Maré and Caju before turning east at São Cristóvão and heading into Centro.

Vincent watched the city flash past as he listened to the banter. He hadn't been to Rio for many years and was surprised by the contrast between then and now. All those years ago it was much poorer, but now he saw evidence of new money wherever he looked. A city on the rise, he thought with appreciation.

Carvalho slowed to handle some traffic in Gamboa and ahead of them he saw Guanabara Bay to the north, reflecting the last of the day's sunshine as twilight enveloped the cityscape. He was jolted from his trance by the sound of screeching brakes and a cacophony of car horns as a jumble of cars nearly collided with one another at a junction. Carvalho gave as good as he got and moved on.

As they turned into Saúde, Carvalho nodded to himself and then raised his forefinger off the wheel, pointing ar the docks. "That's Kruger's boat right there – a Navetta called the Theia. Theia was a Greek goddess," he said. "But that is all they told me."

They slowed down and parked up well away from the Theia. The Brazilian radioed their position to his other men as they watched Kruger's men unloading the loot from his SUV.

They all knew the deal, and that was to ensure the South African and his men on the boat, as well as Corzo, were either taken into custody or taken out altogether. The BOPE force was now in place at the docks so between them all, Reaper was confident the situation could be contained as he saw Dirk Kruger strutting about on the deck.

The South African was holding a cell phone to his face and talking animatedly. Corzo and a few of Kruger's sailors heaved the last of the treasure into the hold and then began smoking at the back of the boat. The Colombian rebel leaned over the stern rail as he watched the water splashing against the hull.

The Frenchman was more hopeful than usual. It was an isolated part of the city well away from the general public and they had many more men than they would need to take on Kruger and his team, not to mention the element of surprise and the home advantage. He hummed a made-up tune as he loaded a mag into the submachine gun and readied the weapon.

"When do we go?" he asked Carvalho.

"When my superiors give the order and not a moment before," came the businesslike reply.

Reaper gave a modest nod. He could live with that, but then with no warning, the Theia jolted forward and began moving away from the docks at full speed. Reaper stared up and saw Kruger in the bridge driving the Navetta out into the bay as its enormous engines were now spewing a tumultuous wake up behind it.

"He's taking it out to sea!" Lexi said.

"This is our last chance to nab the bastard," said Scarlet.

"We have a police boat," Carvalho said. "Don't worry... we'll take it from here, *obrigado*."

"Eh?" Scarlet said. "This is our mission!"

Without warning Ryan snatched Scarlet's weapon and bolted from the Blazer. "I want him dead."

"Ryan!" Scarlet yelled.

Reaper leaped from the Blazer and sprinted after Ryan, but he was already in the police boat and firing her up. He pulled away from the dockside just as Reaper jumped into the boat.

"You could have waited..." he said.

"I can't let him get away," Ryan said coldly. "He has to die, Vincent."

Reaper made no comment, but instead readied his weapon and joined Ryan at the front of the boat. He turned to see the wild flashing of lights as more police pulled up at the docks. "Scarlet and Lexi will not be too happy with you cutting them out of the action."

"You heard Carvalho!" he said, glancing over his shoulder. "He told us he would take it from here. Like hell!"

"Let me get to the helm," the former legionnaire said. "You drive like a girl."

Reaper moved to the wheel and took over control of the small boat, pushing the throttles down as far as they would go and spinning the wheel to correct the course. With peninsulas on the right and the left, Kruger was leaving the last of Rio behind and setting a course across the South Atlantic for Cape Town.

"We don't have much time to catch him!" Ryan said.

Reaper knew boats and he was right. The Theia might have been seaworthy but this little police boat was not. If Kruger got out of the bay and into the ocean he had the fuel, power and resources to cross the entire ocean and get back to South Africa, but they would be going no further than a few miles and then their boat would be little better than driftwood.

"But we have one advantage, mon ami," he said with a grin. 'We have more speed!"

Then the Theia turned hard to starboard to move south around Sugarloaf Mountain before it suddenly lurched violently back to port without warning.

"What the hell are they doing?" Ryan asked.

Then they saw.

Kruger had swerved to avoid a gargantuan container ship which was attempting to enter the bay from the south but the South African was going too fast and crashed into the starboard side of the enormous ship. The captain of the container ship sounded the general alarm to alert the crew to the emergency, but Kruger pushed the Theia through the collision and slipped out the back. They watched the Navetta bobbing around in the container ship's massive wake but Kruger's only response was to order more men to the back and open fire on the police boat.

"Bastard's still going," Reaper said, steering the smaller police boat out to port and giving the container ship the wide berth it deserved.

"But we can't let him get away!" Ryan yelled. "He has the Lost Treasure!"

"But that's not why you want him dead..." Reaper said, giving him a glance.

They drew closer and suddenly other police boats began to swarm around the Navetta.

Reaper fired the first shot, and his bullet was on target. It ploughed into one of Kruger's sailors and spun him around, making him cry out in pain and reach up to the wound.

"Come on, Vincent!" Ryan muttered.

"One more shot..." he said, squinting into his gun sights.

He squeezed the trigger and this time his aim was better. The round tore through the sailor's throat and killed him instantly. He dropped to his knees with a frozen look of stunned terror on his face and then fell forwards over the boarding ramp and disappeared into the black water of Guanabara Bay.

Moments later Reaper was piloting the small police boat up to the stern of the Navetta and he and Ryan were boarding under a hail of fire. A large net was on the deck at the stern, stretched out ready for deployment, but Reaper had his doubts that it was used for fishing.

Before he had a chance to think about it, a man burst out of the cabin at the rear and charged toward them.

Reaper punched the thug in the face with a powerful shovel hook. The man flailed backwards grasping for his weapon but went over the portside rail before he could get hold of it. He plummeted twenty feet into the water and landed on his back in a bloody splash. As a younger man Reaper lived for this sort of adventure, and spent many hours a week working out in the gym to ensure he never came off worse in skirmishes like this, but now he felt his age weighing down on him more and more with each passing year.

Another man stumbled out of the cabin in search of the other sailor and instead found himself directly in between Reaper and Ryan.

Reaper turned to Ryan and the two men exchanged a signal which they both understood at once. Working together they punched the sailor on both sides of his face at the same time which resulted in a terrible crunching sound as he couldn't yield to the strike. He slumped to the floor, face first and was out like a light for the duration. Reaper and Ryan shared a high-five before Carlos Corzo appeared with a hunting knife in his hand and charged toward the Frenchman.

"Get Kruger!" Reaper yelled at Ryan, and threw him the gun. "Three rounds... make them count."

Ryan didn't need to be told twice and ran forward to the wheelhouse. As he went he glanced over his shoulder and saw Reaper and the Colombian rebel fighting hard on the deck. They crashed into the net and began tumbling over each other as the punches flew.

But Ryan couldn't stop to help. He had only one target in mind: Dirk Kruger.

CHAPTER THIRTY-FOUR

Corcovado Mountain is a monumental peak of granite rising nearly two and half thousand feet into the air above the Tijuca Forest to the north of Copacabana. People reached the top via a rack railway which carried them two and half miles to the peak where they could see the world-famous statue of Christ the Redeemer. Nearly one hundred feet tall, the statue had looked over Rio de Janeiro since 1931 and attracted countless millions of tourists.

Now, Ziad Saqqal, Bashir Jawad and Mr Rajavi were scrambling out of the catering truck and running toward their only hope of fulfilling Saqqal's insane plan – the Corcovado Rack Railway. Bursting into the front cab, Saqqal waved a gun in the face of the engineer and forced him to start the train. Jawad followed his boss toward the train while Rajavi sprayed the platform with bullets and then leaped up to join the others. The train began to pull away and start its journey to the peak.

Joe Hawke watched Jawad as he gripped the medical carrying case in his arms the way he might cling to a distressed baby and all around the tourists were screaming and running for cover from Rajavi's submachine gun. They were terrified of the bullets as they fired from the flashing muzzle, but both Hawke and Lea knew they should be a thousand times more terrified of the contents of Jawad's medical case.

"Where the hell are they going?" Lea said.

"This train goes to the top of the mountain," said Hawke. "I think Saqqal wants to release Utopia from an elevation to increase the area the wind spreads it to."

"Which means only one thing…"

"Right – we have a train to catch!"

Hawke and Lea leaped onto the rear car of the rack railway and reloaded their weapons. The train was only two carriages long, and they could see Saqqal holding a gun to the engineer's head up front. Beside him, a nervous Jawad was still gripping the case, but now Rajavi was padding down the first carriage with his submachine gun in his hand.

Hawke frowned. "We could be in trouble. That gun's a lot bigger than mine, Lea."

"Don't worry, baby… it's what you do with it that counts."

He gave her a look and cocked his head at her. "*Is* it now?"

She winked and gave him a kiss on the cheek. "Time to rock n' roll, Josiah."

"Then let's start this dance," he said, and aimed his gun at the man in the mask who was now almost at the door separating the two cars.

Hawke fired, smashing the glass in the door and sending Rajavi diving for cover, but he was soon back up again and returning fire. The bullets from his Heckler & Koch ripped the wooden fittings of the second car to shreds in seconds, showering Hawke and Lea in a cloudburst of splinters and dust.

A nervous Saqqal ordered Rajavi to stop Hawke and Lea from getting to the front of the train under any circumstances. The Iranian's response was to rake the carriage for a second time with his submachine gun, but that was a mistake.

With the H&K out of rounds, Hawke charged forward and grappled the strongman to the floor of the first car. Rajavi fought back like a demon, using the gun as a club and lashing out wildly with the stock, clipping Hawke around the jaw with it.

Hawke flew back, nearly knocked unconscious and Lea charged into the fray in defense of the man she loved. A swift kick sent Rajavi flying backwards where he crashed back into the seats and cracked his head on the steel rim of the window. Hawke got his focus back and leaped on top of the man once again, pulling his fist back and pounding it into the weird silicon mask.

Rajavi flicked his head to the left and right to dodge the blows but he was getting tired. Somehow he got his knees up and managed to wedge his boot in Hawke's stomach and force him back for just enough time to allow Rajavi to get back on his feet.

The Iranian padded forward, his heavy breathing muffled by the silicon mask which was now half-pulled down and at an odd angle. He hurriedly shifted it back but Hawke had stretched it and torn the side during the scuffle and it slipped back down again.

Rajavi slammed him against the top of the chair, squeezing his neck with his enormous hands. Up close, Hawke saw the mask more clearly now, and the hate-filled eyes lurking behind the slits in the silicon. The weirdness was made worse by the mask's low quality. While some silicon masks were almost indistinguishable from real human faces, this was cheap and obvious.

Hawke reached up to grab at the man's hands but he was too strong and his thick, meaty fingers were clasped around the Englishman's windpipe in an iron grip that was impossible to release. Then he had an idea, and moved his hands up from the grip around his throat and onto the mask, grabbing hold of a fistful of silicon at the side of the mask.

Hawke felt the mask come away from the man's face, and Rajavi responded immediately, leaping away and taking a few steps back. He hurried to shift the mask back into place. The terror in his eyes made his fear of exposing his disfigured face to the word harshly obvious.

The former Commando saw his weakness now, and he rushed forward, grabbing a fistful of silicon. This time the mask came away in his hands, and for a second he could hardly believe what he was seeing as he stared into Rajavi's indescribably mutilated face. He was barely recognizable as human, with just the two eyes staring back at him from a mass of scar tissue and exposed teeth and muscle.

Rajavi screamed with rage as the silicon mask flapped away on the breeze and disappeared through the smashed window. He lashed out but his anger destroyed his accuracy and Hawke was able to dodge the blows easily.

Outside the train was rattling around a right-hand bend and then it crossed a wooden bridge. Lea looked down and saw a sheer drop of hundreds of feet falling away from the right-hand side of the tiny rack train.

The Englishman saw the distressed terror in his opponent's eyes, and almost felt sorry for him, but then Rajavi pulled a small flick knife from his pocket and pushed his thumb down on the button. The blade flicked out and flashed in the light.

Rajavi grinned and nodded as he thrust the knife forward, but Hawke was faster.

He grabbed the Iranian's belt and used his own bodyweight against him to push him out of the window.

Rajavi let out a blood-curdling scream as his heavy body tumbled out of the window of the Corcovado rack train and spun over the edge of the cliff. The drop was so far the sound of his screams died out long before he smashed into the bottom.

Hawke dusted his hands off and wiped the blood from his mouth as Lea took a deep breath. They were both aware that the train was now slowing down and looked outside to see they were pulling into the station.

Ahead of them, Saqqal was dragging the engineer out of the front of the train with a knife pushed into his throat. "You come any closer and I slash his throat."

When they were clear, Saqqal pushed the engineer aside and he and Jawad made a break for it, sprinting away from the small station at the top of Corcovado and making their way toward the tourist center at the base of the statue. Christ the Redeemer loomed a hundred feet above their heads as they ran around the base and disappeared to the west side.

Armed only with his old kukri, Hawke and Lea gave chase and pursued the Syrians around to the west side of the Redeemer. When they got to the other side of the platform they were amazed to see the whole of Rio de Janeiro in front of them. It was a breathtaking vista from this elevation, but there was no time to appreciate it because standing at the end of the platform with nothing behind them but a sheer drop of hundreds of feet was General Ziad Saqqal and Dr Jawad, and they were fumbling with the locks on the medical carry case.

"Get back!" Saqqal shouted. "Get back or I will release Utopia!"

"Take it easy, Ziad," Hawke said, slowly reaching around to check the kukri was still on his belt. "You don't want to do that."

"But I do! This is the most lethal airborne plague in history! This, right here in my hands, was responsible for the annihilation of Paititi and the destruction of the

211

Inca civilization. Now it will destroy civilizations again, starting with the people of this city."

"We don't have the NBC suits!" Jawad screamed. "You cannot release it!"

"Silence!"

Jawad made a break for it, and Lea ran after him, leaving Hawke with Saqqal. It didn't take her long to catch up with the unfit scientist, and she brought him down with a leg tackle.

Jawad scrambled to get away from both Lea and Saqqal, desperately trying to flee to safety before Utopia was released and pandemonium broke out in the city. Unlike everyone else on this mountain, he alone knew what would truly happen if this thing somehow got out of containment and was exposed to the atmosphere.

Now, the woman was striking him and trying to stop him getting away. Jawad had never fought in his life, and being struck in the face hurt more than he'd imagined.

"Please stop!" he yelled. "We have to get away! You don't understand!"

Lea stepped back and wiped the blood from her mouth. It was time to shut down the enemy and she knew that when there was serious work to do the time to start was always now. She fired back with a fast palm strike that collided brutally with the scientist's chin, smacking his head back on the concrete and knocking him out.

Then she turned and ran back to Hawke. Somewhere on the other side of the enormous Christ statue he was trying to stop that lunatic Saqqal from releasing the Utopia plague.

*

Ziad Saqqal had no love for humanity, not after what had happened to his family in the rocket attack, and he had made his peace with the universe. He had wondered if he could live with himself and unleash the plague on the world at the same time, and he had thought yes. Now he had to consider if he could take his own life in the process.

Staring at the former SBS man who was now fast approaching him, he thought yes once again, and began to unlock the carrying case. Dying in agony from Utopia over the next few hours would be preferable to a life in jail on terror charges.

But then the Englishman pulled a chunky knife from his belt and hurled it at him. It flew through the air with the speed of a Ninja's shuriken and he felt the heavy blade plunge into his chest. His eyes widened like two saucers as he realized what had happened, and then he turned those two crazed eyes downwards to the wound and saw the mighty blade sticking through his ribs.

He could feel the case in his hand as he began to go over the rail. If he hurled himself off, Utopia would be released before the English bastard could stop it. It was his last chance... his last act. He felt his consciousness slipping away as the blood poured from the terrible wound in his chest and pump over his body.

Hawke watched as Saqqal began to topple over the rail, the case still in his hand. If it went over the cliff with the Syrian it would smash apart and Utopia would be released to the world, furiously multiplying as it spread its death cloud over the human population, spreading from city to city.

He knew he had only one chance to stop this, and sprinted forward with all his might. With his body awash with adrenalin he surged forward and snatched the medical case just as Saqqal toppled over the edge.

213

*

He peered over the cliff edge and saw the smashed body of Ziad Saqqal crash into the rocks and spin down in to the ravine, broken and bashed beyond repair. He breathed out with relief as he locked the carry case back up and set it down on the concrete, and then he felt Lea slide her arm through his. He turned as she kissed him on the cheek, the enormous statue of Christ the Reedeemer rising above them.

They kissed for a moment and hugged each other before returning their gaze to the incredible sight of Rio de Janeiro. The city lights began to sparkle as night approached.

"That is one pretty view, Josiah."

"Thanks, I'm trying something new with my hair."

"Not you, ya fool – the city behind your big, fat head."

"Ah…"

Lea rolled her eyes and pointed to an enormous, steep peak jutting out into Guanabara Bay. "What's that mountain over there?"

"Sugarloaf Mountain. If old Saqqal had gone there instead we could have re-enacted Moonraker," Hawke said with a devilish grin.

"Cable cars… really?" Lea said. "After Switzerland and Zaugg?"

"Yeah… maybe not."

She peered over the rail and saw the flashing lights as the police raced up the hill. "Can't be too long till we have company."

"Hmm – shame I don't have my wingsuit. This would make the perfect launching platform, but as it is, we've got quite the walk ahead of us so let's get started."

214

Lea cocked her head and squinted as she looked at his stomach. "She's right you know."

"Who's right?"

"Cairo. She said you were getting a bit of a tummy."

"Are you having a laugh?"

"Sure I am."

He smiled. Having a laugh was always easy if Lea Donovan was around.

CHAPTER THIRTY-FIVE

Ryan Bale wiped the sweat from his forehead and checked the magazine Reaper had given him. Three rounds. He smacked it back into the grip of the Glock.

Make them count.

After a lifetime looking down his nose at violence and guns, it suddenly felt good in his hands. He liked the weight of it, the shape of the grip, the feel of the steel trigger guard.

The power of life and death.

His new-found love of the weapon mixed dangerously with the deep hatred he felt for Dirk Kruger, the man who had kidnapped him and dragged him halfway around the world. The man who had used him like a walking encylopaedia, the man who had kept him gagged with his hands behind his back so he could use him as a bargaining chip in case ECHO got in his way again.

The man who was trapped on this boat with him... and now he was going to kill him stone dead.

Ryan crept along the portside deck, gun raised into the aim. He heard firing and ducked inside a doorway for cover, but then he realized he wasn't the target because he could still hear shooting.

He moved forward to see Kruger blasting the hell out of the throttle controls and the boat slowed rapidly in response. The South African turned and saw him, and immediately fired on him. The bullets were wide, and pinged off the bulkhead in a shower of sparks, leaving

Ryan diving for cover behind the portside wall of the wheelhouse.

He scrambled to safety and remembered once again he had only three bullets.

Make them count.

*

Reaper felt the water rush over him as he hit the ocean. The two men had become tangled in Kruger's next and as they rolled off the boat into the sea the Frenchman suddenly understood what the South African used it for – torturing and killing his enemies.

As they went out behind the Navetta the boat dragged them along in its wake, and Corzo now started punching him hard in the face. Reaper knew only one man was getting out of this net alive, and it wasn't going to be Carlos Corzo.

He tried to dodge the punches but the net was tangled around his neck and he found it almost impossible to move... and now they were sinking under the surface and struggling to take their last gasp of air before being totally submerged.

And now they were under.

Reaper managed to wrench his right arm free of the net and grab Corzo's throat. He squeezed hard until he could see his eyes bulging in his skull. It wasn't hard, when it came down to it. All he had to do was think about his twin boys back in Provence growing up without a father while this piece of shit walked the streets with a panatella hanging off his smirking lip. That was enough to find what needed to be found to take Corzo out of the game.

But Corzo wasn't going to go down without a fight, and he forced Reaper's hand away before wildly grabbing a fistful of the nylon net in both hands and forcing it down over his opponent's face. He pushed down hard as if he were running a wire through a block of cheese and Reaper felt the sharp nylon cords pushing into his face, dragging down hard at the corners of his mouth and gouging the bridge of his nose.

He screamed in pain but all that came out was the air he had been trapping in his lungs. It burst from his mouth in an explosion of bubbles as he fought to get the net off his face, but now Corzo was wrapping it around his neck. The cord coiled around his neck like a snake and he felt it pushing down on his Adam's apple. It was now he considered that he couldn't breathe anyway because of the sea, but Corzo was making damn sure he never breathed again.

Slowly, Reaper felt his world turning black. Time was running out.

*

Ryan fired the Glock at Kruger but the round ricocheted off the control panel and lodged in the roof.

Only two bullets left.

The South African darted for the door, only just getting through before the London dropout fired another shot which also narrowly missed. It felt good, he thought, to send this man scuttling away like the stinking rat he truly was…

"I see the boy becomes a man!" Kruger called through the wheelhouse door. He raised his gun and returned fire at Ryan.

Ryan slammed himself back against the steel wall on the other side of the wheelhouse and took a deep breath.

One bullet left.

Was he doing the right thing? Maybe he just didn't have it in him... now Kruger was fighting back and he was alone. Joe and Lea were lost in Rio somewhere hunting Saqqal and Jawad down and Lexi and Scarlet were back in the docks. As for Reaper, the last time he'd seen him he was on the back of the boat locked in hand-to-hand combat with Carlos Corzo. As far as Ryan Bale was concerned, now it was just him and Dirk Kruger... mano a mano. He started to doubt if he had it in him.

"Come on you little weasel!" Kruger shouted. He laughed. "Show yourself!"

Ryan took another deep breath and readied himself. He stared up at the sky. Felt the cold steel of the wheelhouse through his mess of hair. Felt the sea breeze coming in off the South Atlantic. Heard the low rumbling of the trawler's diesel engine somewhere beneath him.

He checked his gun had that one last round in the chamber for the third time and counted to five before spinning around the bulkhead door and aiming the gun at Kruger.

But he was gone.

He ran over to where the South African had been taking cover but there was nothing there except a few empty cartridges. Then he saw a flash of movement in his peripheral vision and flicked his head to the right to see Kruger jogging down the stairs leading to the lower deck on the starboard side.

Ryan gave chase, feeling the thrill of the hunt for the first time. He was now hunting Kruger – a man who had kept him captive and threatened him with death – and the prospect of taking his revenge was like electricity coursing through his veins. He pounded down the metal steps only to see his enemy darting inside the Navetta, but made the decision to pursue the hunt until the very end.

Inside now, and then he heard the revving of an engine coming from the other side of the boat. Stupidly, he thought for a split second that it was a motorbike but he didn't work out the truth until a second too late when he emerged on the deck and saw Dirk Kruger racing away from the Navetta on a black Jet Ski. He crossed in front of the bow and sped away into the twilight.

Ryan sprinted back to the rail on the starboard side and raised his gun. Kruger was in range, and even though he was swerving from side to side, he knew he could take him out. He moved his gun from side to side as he tracked the fleeing South African and then he got the man's head in his sights.

He paused, slowed his breathing and started to squeeze the trigger.

And then he fired.

He lowered his head when he realized he had missed the shot.

*

Vincent Reno felt his life slipping away and knew he had to act now or it would all be over. With no more oxygen, his head was spinning and he was losing his vision. He searched himself for any energy he had left and used his last reserves to wrench Corzo's hands away from the net and then he hooked his thumbs into the Colombian's eyes and pushed as hard as he could.

Corzo's screams made the seawater white with bubbles and he instinctively swam back from Reaper and raised his hands to his eyes. It was the only chance Reaper needed, and he seized the moment. With Corzo still blinded by his attack, Reaper pulled himself free of the net and wrapped it around the Colombian's arms and legs, tying him inextricably into the tangles of the net.

Corzo lashed out blindly, but missed the former legionnaire who dodged the blows and then used his opponent's bound body as a ladder to haul himself up out of the water. With the Navetta chugging out to sea ahead of him, he pulled himself up the netting until he was clear of the water and then snatched Corzo's bowie knife off the deck. He slashed the netting until it was no longer connected to the boat and it rapidly disappeared in the Navetta's wake.

Reaper heaved the air into his lungs as he watched the Colombian thrashing about in the net in the middle of Guanabara Bay, but then he was still, and there was nothing more to be done.

The Frenchman dropped the knife and jogged up the deck toward the wheelhouse, and it was then he saw Ryan Bale aiming his gun at Kruger who was fleeing on a chunky Jet Ski. He paused a heartbeat longer than a trained soldier and the shot went low, smacking into the machine's foamy wake, and then the target disappeared behind the peninsula.

*

Ryan Bale's heart sank as he watched Dirk Kruger tearing away from the Navetta on the Jet Ski. It was a Kawasaki Ultra 310, the most powerful on the market, and now the South African was revving the 1.5 litre engine to its max as he ripped across the surface of Guanabara Bay.

Reaper was pounding along the starboard deck now, and Ryan was relieved to see he was okay, but as Kruger rapidly disappeared into the twilight on his way to the coast, Ryan dropped his head again, dropped the gun and cursed himself for losing his nerve and failing to kill the man. He knew Hawke or Lea or any of the others wouldn't have paused like that, and it was in that half-second that a human life was taken or saved.

"He got away," Ryan said. "I tried to take a shot but I missed."

"You did your best, Ryan," Reaper said, understanding immediately what had happened. The boy had lost his nerve and paused for a second too long, letting Kruger get away. It wasn't his fault. Not everyone had it in them.

Reaper patted him on the shoulder and rolled a cigarette. "We need to get back to shore."

They took the Navetta back to the coast where they saw their friends on the dock surrounded by flashing lights and emergency services vehicles. Carvalho was leaning on the hood of his car and looking pretty angry. A few yards to his left Hawke and Lea were pulling up in a cab and now they were walking over to Scarlet and Lexi.

As Reaper and Ryan stepped off the Navetta they watched three black Escalades approach from the road to the north and then pull up alongside the dock.

Eddie Kosinski climbed out the back of the first Escalade and flashed his badge at Carvalho. The police sergeant was clearly expecting him and immediately waved him and his men through the cordon.

He marched up to the ECHO team as bold as brass and ran a hand over his stubble. "Pretty down these parts, huh?"

"Why are you here, Kosinski?" Hawke said. "

"A little bird tipped me off that there was something going down in Rio and you know what I did?"

Scarlet stared at him. "Tried to buy a personality online but couldn't find any that fit your ego?"

"No – and that's not funny by the way. What I did was get a few buddies together and come down here for a long weekend. You don't mind if I join you now, right?"

"Who's pulling your strings, Kosinski?" Hawke said, taking a step closer and squaring up to him.

"You know that saying about the world being on turtles all the way down? Well with me it's bosses all the way up, Hawke. You know how it is."

"If you want the man who tried to loot the Lost City," Lea said, "he's on a Jet Ski in that direction."

Kosinski grinned. "Just leave that to us…"

"You don't seem to be in much of a hurry to catch the bad guys," Scarlet said.

It was clear whoever had sent the CIA down here knew a hell of a lot about what was going on, and Kosinski's 'little bird' reference was a cheap shot trying to make him think Alex had been the leak. Hawke grinned, knowing how satisfying it was going to be when he finally crushed Eddie Kosinski. "You know, if I didn't know any better I'd say you're deliberately letting Dirk Kruger get away tonight."

"Like you said, you don't know any better."

Kosinski gave them a sarcastic smile and walked over to the Navetta. "If you don't mind, I have an ancient lost treasure to inventory."

The ECHO team walked along the docks and looked back at Kosinski and his men as they removed the treasure from the Theia.

"We need to get to the bottom of Eddie Kosinski," Hawke said. He crossed his arms and perched on the edge of a dock piling. "What do we know about him?"

"He's smug," Lea said.

"And a bastard," said Scarlet.

Lexi sighed. "And he gets the better of us too many times."

"And he's CIA," Reaper said.

"Right – so he's working for someone at the CIA who knows about Dirk Kruger and his activities," Hawke said.

Scarlet blew out some smoke and looked up at the stars. "Not to mention all that immortality stuff."

"I think we need Alex to start digging round Langley," Lea said.

"Agreed," Hawke said. "She's very good at that."

Scarlet let out a heavy sigh and casually flicked her cigarette butt into the sea. "Come on, you bastards. Let's go and get a drink."

CHAPTER THIRTY-SIX

Tiger looked at Pig and Pig looked at Tiger. Neither man knew the other's name, and that was how it had always been done. Neither knew where the other lived and neither wanted to know. They were not bloody-thirsty, undisciplined gangsters but highly-trained public servants with a job to do. It might be a dirty job, but someone had to do it, and that someone was Tiger and his associates.

Unlike Tiger, Pig was nearing retirement and looking forward to a generous pension which he planned to spend in Zhuhai with his wife. The prefecture-level city was in the subtropical south but the South China Sea kept the temperatures down. It was the perfect place to retire. Just one more job to do and he would punch out and leave the Ministry behind for the rest of his life.

"Who?" was all Pig said. A visit from Tiger could mean only thing and it wasn't to play wǔzǐqí.

Tiger said nothing but slid the manila folder across the table.

Pig glanced from the folder back to Tiger and then back down before gently lifting the cover. He raised his eyebrows and then sucked in his lips. "I see."

"Zhou wants it done in a hurry."

"Zhou can take a shit in a hurry," Pig said. "A job like this takes time and careful planning."

Tiger nodded. He was thinking the same thing.

"Who else have you in mind?"

"Rat."

"Inevitable, of course."

225

"And Monkey."

Pig nodded his head and after taking another lingering glance inside the folder closed it back up. "He'll have to be watched."

"I can handle him."

Pig nodded. "She's aged well. Seems a shame."

"She's got new friends now. Likes to play games in the West."

Another tired nod. Tiger wondered if he was keeping the other man away from his bed.

"Where is she?"

"Rio de Janeiro. We don't know why."

"When do we go after her?"

"As soon as we get the others. Do you know where they are?"

"Rat is where he always is," Pig said with a yawn, and pushed his chopsticks back into his soybean noodles. "I dread to think where we'll find Monkey." He deftly pulled out a string of the wheat noodles and twirled them around to gather more of the zhajiang sauce. Then he pinched some of the stir-fried beef and dipped it into the salty soybean paste before passing the whole bundle into his mouth.

"How's the meat?" Tiger asked.

Pig wiped his mouth with a napkin and nodded vehemently. "Delicious."

The beef was always delicious here.

And Agent Dragonfly's days were numbered.

CHAPTER THIRTY-SEVEN

Copacabana

"You win some, you lose some."

Hawke downed his lager and put the glass on the table with a loud smack. "Maybe, Lexi," he said. "But you don't lose against a man like Dirk Kruger. We've had too many losses. We let Mendoza get away in Mexico – and look at the carnage that mistake cost. We lost Maria and maybe even Rich, and now we let the man responsible for most of that slip through our fingers like sand."

Ryan took a sip of the lager. "On the bright side, I'm still here. That's how come we didn't get Kruger. None of you would have screwed that up."

Scarlet laughed loudly but immediately stopped, glancing at Ryan. "You've changed."

"Have I?"

She nodded. "You're now half-nerd, half-man."

"Well the nerd half wants a cigarette," Ryan said, and helped himself to one from Scarlet's pack. He put it in his mouth and fired it up with her Zippo. Everyone stared at him as he blew the smoke out into the air and sighed.

Lea looked concerned. "Are you okay, Ry?"

He gave her a sharp look. "Sure, why wouldn't I be?"

"You don't smoke cigarettes, for one thing."

Ryan downed his beer and took another drag. "I smoke weed all the time, so what's the difference?" He shrugged his shoulders and fixed his eyes on her. She could see something was missing now. She knew he was still in shock from the news of Maria's death, but this seemed like something else, something more... he had a new look in his eyes, a new recklessness she had never seen before.

"Just sayin'..."

Hawke broke the tension by rising from his chair and asking anyone if they wanted another beer. The consensus was clear, so he stepped inside for a few moments. He emerged a few minutes later and pulled his chair out. He sat down with a sigh and handed around the cold beers. The mission had been successful – to a degree. They had ended Saqqal's insane bioweapon threat and passed the Utopia plague to the authorities, and they had also stopped Kruger from stealing the Lost Treasure of the Incas, but they had lost it all to Eddie Kosinski. Someone had tipped him off and his CIA boys had been all over the Rio docks like white on rice. It wasn't the first time he had lost the grand prize to Kosinski.

The food Lea had ordered arrived at their table – flame-grilled picanha steaks with black beans and rice, and another round of chilled Brahmas on the side. He took a slow sip of the cold beer and glanced out across Copacabana Beach and the South Atlantic Ocean beyond. Down here in the southern hemisphere it was summer, and the tropical heat of the bay enveloped him like a blanket.

Above him, the stars struggled to be seen through the incredible light pollution of the behemoth city at his back, but he could still see a few in the far eastern sky. He ate some of the steak and tried to relax, but what would have been a perfect evening was destroyed by the absence of Maria, Rich and Alex and he knew everyone here tonight felt the same way. The only consolation was

Scarlet hadn't made any crappy Barry Manilow jokes since they'd arrived at the restaurant.

He tried to shake the thought of their missing friends from his mind, but it lingered like cannon smoke on a battlefield. He lifted his first bottle and finished the beer before picking up the second and taking the top third off in a couple of seconds. He set it down and looked around the small, beleaguered group.

"I think we won today," Reaper said, but without conviction.

"How'd you work that out?" Lea said.

He gave his usual shrug. "We discovered the Lost City of the Incas for one thing, and we stopped Kruger getting the treasure," he said matter-of-factly. He took a long drag on his roll-up cigarette and winced as he sucked the smoke down. When he spoke next, the smoke tumbled out with his words. "And we ended the threat of Saqqal and Jawad," he said, tapping his forefinger on the table to underline the point.

"I guess, but it still feels like a failure," Lea said.

"And we all know why," Ryan said.

"Nevertheless," Scarlet threw in. "We won the battle we set out to win."

Hawke shook his head. "We might have won the battle, but we're losing the war. Our team is in shreds and Elysium is smouldering ruins."

"We *will* win, Joe," Lea said.

"We've got a lot of work to do, Lea," he said.

The others nodded in agreement. They all knew what was expected of them. With Eden out of the game and no way to know when or even if he would be back, they all had to give more to the cause, but they all knew how hard it would be.

Hawke unbuttoned the top of his shirt and Scarlet wolf-whistled loudly causing a few of the diners to turn and gawp.

"Weyhay!" she said. "Undo another couple of buttons just for me will you, darling?"

He gave her a sarcastic smirk.

"And if you pop open the top of your shorts you can let that gut out for a few minutes."

Hawke stared at her and after a long period of silence a thin, uncertain smile broke out on his face. They had a lot of work to do – hunting down Dirk Kruger for a start, not to mention smashing the Oracle and his sinister cult – but he had the camaraderie of the people sitting around this table... the camaraderie of his closest friends, and nothing could beat that. He raised his bottle over the center of the table.

"To revenge?" Scarlet said with a dark sparkle in her eyes.

"No," Hawke said with a solemn shake of his head. "To old friends and new adventures."

EPILOGUE

Galway Bay

Maggie Donovan liked to watch the weather coming in. It was one of the few things she could do at her age that didn't make her bones ache and her eyelids heavy. Today was not disappointing. Everyone at the Haven Bay Nursing Home had been following the storm out in the Atlantic these last few days. It looked like a nasty one, and she pitied anyone caught out in it.

Now, the water in the bay was churning under a leaden sky and the coast guard had warned the trawlermen to come in, but it was warm and cosy in Maggie's soft chair, and she celebrated the fact with a small glass of whiskey. She liked it without fuss, which the staff knew meant neat and at least three fingers high or it got sent back. She liked Tyrconnell, or maybe even Connemara peated malt, but that only happened if family brought it in. Usually she had to live with a blend.

"How are you this afternoon, Maggie?"

Maggie turned to see Grace enter the room. She liked Grace because she always plumped her cushions when she talked to her and today was no exception.

"I'm fine dear."

"Are all your family coming in, Maggie? It's not every day you turn ninety, after all."

"Most but not all," Maggie said with a hint of sadness. "My sister won't be visiting."

"Ah – your sister," Grace said sympathetically. They'd all heard about the sister. Many of the staff thought it meant Maggie's mind was finally going, but ninety was a good innings so it didn't raise too much concern. "And how is Lea?"

"I haven't seen her for a long time. It's very sad."

Maggie opened the drawer and pulled out the picture. She bumped her wrist on the wood on the way out and cursed with the pain. Her skin was like cigarette paper these days and she was lucky it hadn't broken open again. "Here she is."

Grace took the picture and smiled. "She sure is beautiful, Maggie. I'll give you that."

"Isn't she just?" she said, beaming with pride.

"But she can't be older than thirty."

"I'd say about that yes, but my memory's not what it was when I was eighty, you know."

"Are you sure she's not your granddaughter?" Grace asked quietly as she put the cushion back behind Maggie. "She must be sixty years younger than you."

"Of course I'm sure!"

Grace gave another sympathetic smile and handed the picture back to Maggie, who looked at it long enough for a tear to appear in her eye, and then she put it back in the drawer.

"We'll be having the party in the recreation room, Maggie. Is that all right?"

Maggie nodded, but said nothing. The storm was in now, and starting to whip up on the shale cliffs of the bay.

Grace moved to the door and turned down the dimmer-switch on the light. "I can't tell you the details but some of the guests have a secret planned for you, is that all right?" A gentle pink glow fell over the room, and for a few moments the only sound was the quiet sound of ticking as the radiator pipes expanded under the floorboards.

"Oh yes," Maggie said, a smile breaking through the wrinkles on her face. "I've lived with secrets all my life."

THE END

AUTHOR'S NOTE

I hope you enjoyed reading this book as much as I enjoyed writing it. I wanted a lean, fast story so I hope I achieved that with this. I started researching the Incas and putting this story together a while ago when I was planning *The Aztec Prophecy*, and because of the cliffhanger in *The Secret of Atlantis* I made the decision to release them together so you didn't have to wait ages to find out what happened! These books take many weeks to write (sometimes longer…) so sadly I cannot promise another Hawke adventure for a while…

Let me use this place to thank you for all the support I receive in my emails and to say that I always reply to messages even if takes me a few days. Coming up next is a real change with the release of a standalone action-adventure thriller called *The Armageddon Protocol* which is not in the Hawke universe and features a new set of characters that I really hope you'll enjoy.

Beyond that I will be trying hard to bring *The Sword of Fire (Joe Hawke #9)* together for a spring 2017 release, and stay tuned for some big changes that are coming next year! With that said and done let me wish you, Dear Mystery Reader, a very Merry Christmas and a Happy New Year for 2017. Scarlet's coming over to mine this year and she's demanding a drinking competition with me. Oh dear…

Rob

The Joe Hawke Series

The Vault of Poseidon (Joe Hawke #1)
Thunder God (Joe Hawke #2)
The Tomb of Eternity (Joe Hawke #3)
The Curse of Medusa (Joe Hawke #4)
Valhalla Gold (Joe Hawke #5)
The Aztec Prophecy (Joe Hawke #6)
The Secret of Atlantis (Joe Hawke #7)
The Lost City (Joe Hawke #8)

The Sword of Fire (Joe Hawke #9) is scheduled
for release in the spring of 2017

**For free stories, regular news and updates,
please join my Facebook page**

https://www.facebook.com/RobJonesNovels/

Or Twitter

@AuthorRobJones

Made in the USA
Lexington, KY
09 January 2017